Secretary to the Orc

LYONNE RILEY

STORY INTRODUCTION

Rosette Kristoff is impeccable at her job, but there's just one problem: she has a massive crush on her orc boss, Mr. Vincent Roth. Though he appreciates what she has on offer, he never touches, much to her indignation.

That is, until Vincent discovers Rosette's after-hours job working at a gentlemen's sex club as "Velvet." Then all his pent-up hunger for his beautiful assistant erupts, and he finally crosses the line.

But a relationship between them is a recipe for Human Resources disaster, and Vincent knows it can't be more than a tryst at a club. The last thing he needs is to form a mate bond.

Once he gets a taste of Velvet, though, can Vincent really stay away from Rosette?

CONTENT WARNINGS

May contain spoilers!

- Graphic depictions of sex
- Power imbalances
- Sex work
- Flashing
- Sex in the workplace
- Degradation
- Voyeurism
- Public/stage sex
- Public nudity and bathing

CHAPTER
ONE

ROSETTE

It's a fine Thursday morning, and I'm excited to go to work today. I had a very good idea last night, and I can't wait to try it out.

As always, at nine a.m., a black SUV pulls up to the curb in front of my apartment building. I open the back door and slide inside. Across the console sits my boss, Mr. Roth.

Vincent Roth is big, even for an orc, with dark hair cut close to his head and wearing an impenetrable pair of sunglasses. His shoulders are so broad and square, his body so dense, it's like he's made of concrete. His belly is big, but not in the way that makes him appear fat—it's more a layer of protection over his thick mus-culature.

He must work out a ton to have a body like that.

Today, we're on our way to get some coffee before heading to a prospective site. The car pulls into the fifteen-minute parking zone, then I head in to grab our orders, which I placed on-line. The drinks are waiting under Mr. Roth's name. I snatch them up before heading back out to the car. He takes his, nodding and saying nothing as I get back in and the driver pulls away from the curb.

Not even a *thank you*. Silence, like always. But he does stare at me, his eyes traveling up from my belly to my tits, where I've left the top two buttons of my silk top open.

Once he's finished eye-fucking me, he *smirks*, bringing his tusk up his cheek. They're menac-ing, those sharp, white tusks, even more so when he smiles like that. I despise that smug look, when he sees through me.

Because he knows I like it. When I bend over to pick up a pen, he peers at my ass, just as I'd hoped. While I lean forward to take a sip of my drink at lunch, his eyes drop to the collar of my shirt, appreciating my offerings. Even when he interviewed me, I could feel his eyes all over my body. I know I have great tits, and definitely a round, defined butt—especially so in my tight pencil skirts and silky work blouses.

He always looks. Peruses. Openly staring.

Mr. Roth only comes into the office for a few hours a week, and the rest of the time, I need to tag along wherever he chooses to go. He goes to bars, meets with clients there, then visits a work site. Then he meets with another client, only returning to the office to tidy things up.

All day, we travel side by side in the back of his black SUV, me with my notebook and phone, taking calls, making appointments, canceling them when a lunch goes too long and trying to reschedule. All, of course, while Mr. Roth stares. While he undresses me with his eyes. While he blatantly looks from my feet, up my thighs, to my skirt and tits before meeting my face.

But never once has he touched me. Never has he behaved inappropriately. And that's what I can't stand. He objectifies me with his gaze while refusing to ever cross the line. I don't even think he's brushed my hand by accident at a restaurant. He's certainly never pinched my ass or found an excuse to feel up my tits. I haven't even felt the brush of his hip in the car. He always keeps a good foot of distance between us, even though he takes up most of the back seat.

And I'm tired of it. Today, I have a surprise for him. Maybe it will finally turn the tide.

When we reach the first work site, I hop out first with my notebook and pen ready to go, my blonde hair neatly tucked in a high bun. I go for a more natural look with my makeup to blend in.

Slowly the other car door opens, and Mr. Roth gets out. He has to stoop, but when he emerges, he towers above me.

"Come," he says, tucking his hands into his pockets as we head toward the site. The foreman comes out to greet us and starts showing us around. I take copious notes. Mr. Roth is interested in investing in this new high-rise, but it has to make sense for the firm financially. I don't handle that part.

Mr. Roth doesn't need to tell me anymore what to write down. I know what he's interested in here—the vision, the exclusivity that would make these apartments more valuable than others in the city, the access and amenities. Right now, it's little more than an empty lot, but it could become something greater.

When we're done here, it's back in the car to the office for a meeting. I go through the notes I took earlier and transcribe them, then email them to Mr. Roth. I can see when he gets the message during his meeting, because he glances down at his phone, nods to me through the glass window, then turns his attention back to the CEO.

Afterward, we're off to a client lunch where once more, I take notes as they talk, forgotten at the side of the table. When the waiter comes, Mr. Roth doesn't ask me what I want to eat.

"A Caesar salad with grilled chicken for her," he says, then moves on with the conversation.

I don't object. I've never objected. Mr. Roth has ordered for me since the first lunch we ever had, asking for the same thing each time. Every restaurant has Caesar salad, after all.

Sometimes I think about telling him I want a sandwich, but I don't. He also orders me the sparkling water, and then I don't have to say a word for the entire lunch.

From time to time, a client will introduce themselves to me. I always shake hands and say my name back, but that's the extent of it. Mr. Roth makes it clear that they aren't to talk to me.

And then it's back in the car, where I can feel his yellow gaze raking over me. He simply stares as we drive, occasionally licking his lips. I feel almost naked by the time we get back to the office.

Once Mr. Roth is seated, he turns on the phone and dials in to a conference call while I walk to the cooler for a cup of water. He watches me as he talks, unabashedly staring at my ass when I return to my desk. It's time for my surprise.

"Please remind the shareholders once more that these are long-term projects," Mr. Roth says into the speaker. "It will take some time for revenue to—"

As I navigate into my chair, I slide my legs apart. I didn't wear underwear today, and I just gave him a full look at the goods underneath my skirt.

His eyes get bigger, but he manages to continue without interruption. "—start trickling in."

The rest of the call is uneventful, but Mr. Roth's eyes on me are like molten lava. I wonder if I've finally turned the corner.

But at the end of the day, nothing has changed when the car pulls up in front of my apartment. Mr. Roth's eyes travel from my face, down to my chest, over my cleavage to my kept nails. I'm close enough to him that he could easily reach out and touch me if he wanted.

"Have a good night, Ms. Kristoff," he says in that deep, booming voice. I don't know if he's spoken to me directly like this all day. But he doesn't move his hand, either.

I nod as I get out, disappointed once again. "Thank you, Mr. Roth." I close the door, and the car pulls away.

But then it's time to get ready for my after-hours job, where I can finally have all the things Mr. Roth denies me.

I only work my second gig three nights a week—Thursday, Friday, and Saturday. Sunday is my true day off, the one I take to get my nails done. I do a facial when I can, and every two months, I stop in for a new cut and dye. Then I go on a run and get ready for the week.

Tonight's Thursday, which means the lounge will be quieter than it is on the weekends. Still, I have some regulars who come in specifically looking for me on our less busy nights so they can catch me before I'm otherwise occupied.

After showering, I head to Octavio's. It's a

club on the top floor, with a bar area and dance floor. Downstairs, though, is a place far less well-known. That's where I work, hosting gentlemen who are looking for a more lascivious activity.

Two other girls are in the dressing room when I arrive.

"Hey, Velvet," they greet me. We all use pseudonyms here, and I always try to wear at least one piece of velvet on me as part of the gag. Tonight, I'm in a scarlet velvet skirt barely covering my ass, garter belts holding up black fishnets, with a lacy black and red corset. I ask one of my coworkers to tie it up for me, then spray on a bit of my favorite perfume before heading out onto the floor.

There are waiters working, but our clients always prefer it when we bring them their drinks. I scan the lounge to see who's here, recognizing only one familiar face: Elias, the manticore who comes in from time to time and likes when I serve him. But he's already occupied with Bunny, a tiny little Asian woman sitting on his lap with her bare tits in his hands.

Guess Elias won't need me tonight.

Other groups of people are talking and drinking, already with women at their tables. I pass Veronica moaning as a man and a woman sit together, fingering her. Down the hallway, where the private rooms are, I can hear another one of my coworkers cry out in carnal bliss.

But no one flags me down as I pass. Unusual. So I head to the bar and check in with Matt to see who might be in need of my attentions.

"We have a new guy," Matt says, pointing around the corner. "In the VIP section. You should go welcome him. Maybe pick up a fresh client."

I like the sound of that. Making a first impression is how you get a regular, and it's a bonus if it's somebody rich enough for the VIP section.

With a quick thanks, I beeline around the end of the bar for the smaller VIP room. The bouncer nods at me as I pass.

It's quiet in here, with only three people present—two old men drinking whiskey, and then one man with his back facing me. I nod and smile at the two men, who give me cursory nods back before returning to their conversation.

Not interested. My new guy must be this massive pair of shoulders in front of me.

Wait. I recognize those exact shoulders, that perfectly tailored suit.

Mr. Roth. Mr. Vincent Roth is in my place of work. And he hasn't seen me yet.

I freeze in my spot, then start to back away. If he doesn't look up from the menu he's studying, then he won't see me. I can get out of here, maybe pretend I'm sick, and go home before my boss even catches wind of it.

I can't have him find out about this. Would he ever look at me the same way again if he knew this is what I do in my off-time? If he knew I let strangers fondle me, sometimes even take me away to back rooms with locked doors?

I'm almost to the entry to the VIP lounge when suddenly, Mr. Roth's head shoots up. He turns in his chair, his nostrils flared—and just like that, his yellow eyes connect with mine from across the room.

Instantly, I stop moving, like a deer caught in headlights. I'm so fucked.

For the first time since I've met him, I think Mr. Roth genuinely looks surprised. I've never seen him caught off guard before, with his lips parted, his brows raised.

There's nothing I can do now that he's seen me, but I can't react. This place is supposed to be anonymous, professional. I have to pretend that I don't know him, that I've never seen him before in my life. I have to treat him like any other client.

Getting my wits back about me, I slide easily into customer service mode, approaching the table and then leaning forward over it to give him a good view of my cleavage inside the corset.

"Good evening, sir," I say in a sultry voice, the way I would with anyone at the lounge. "I'm Velvet. Would you like a drink to start?"

Mr. Roth stares at me, his eyes never once straying down to my tits, which are still on display for him.

"Miss..." he begins, then stops himself. I pray silently that he doesn't try to use my real name here. His eyes search mine, his thick eyebrows furrowed.

After a heavy moment, he finally says, "I would enjoy a drink, *Velvet*."

I put a hand on his back, gentle and inviting. "Tell me what you want, sir, and it's all yours."

CHAPTER
TWO

VINCENT

've heard rumors about the secret lounge under Octavio's for some time, but it had never truly interested me before. I am a wealthy orc, with decent looks and at least a modicum of charm when I turn it on. Finding someone to fondle or fuck has never been an issue for me if I actively look for it.

But I haven't looked in a long time, not since I hired Ms. Kristoff.

Rosette. I would never say it out loud, her first name. I think I'd get an erection instantly if I did. No, since the moment I brought her on—my little blonde human assistant, with her big eyes and soft makeup—I can't think about anyone else.

I jack off every morning and night to the thought of her, to the image of her big tits straining the buttons of her silk blouse, her toned ass moving with every stride under her skirt. It's never too short, never a question of her professionalism, and yet it's deeply erotic to see the clear outline of each ass cheek, even the indent where her thong underwear wraps around her plump hips.

Everything about her is goddamned perfect. She's small by virtue of being human, but for a human, she has meat on her, just the right amount. She wouldn't break under my big hands, and she might even be able to take my cock if I taught her body how.

But I can't have Ms. Kristoff. I will never give her what she wants, not while she works for me. It's too much of a hassle, too big of an HR nightmare. And until recently, I've survived the way she shows off all her incredible assets, simply begging me to reach out and squeeze that marvelous butt. It's been two years now since bringing her on, which is two years since I've had sex with anyone. Sometimes it feels like my dick's going to fall off.

Still, I'd never fire her. It would be impossible to find someone else who knows how to do her job as well as she does it—silently, with laser precision. Ms. Kristoff knows my mind, what I want out of her, and she executes it without requiring intervention or correction.

Today though, I finally reached my limit. After she showed off what she has between her legs, bare and exposed for my eyes, all I wanted was to grab her and plant her on my lap, rip off her skirt, unzip my pants and bury my cock in her. The need became so overwhelming when she said goodbye that I realized...

I needed to move on with my life. I needed to get some kind of relief with a warm body and try to banish this obsession from my mind, because it will never go anywhere as long as Ms. Kristoff works for me. I can't have her, no matter how soft and delectable her pussy looked between her toned thighs.

So tonight, I decided to give up on her once and for all and do something about this insatiable hunger. Octavio's is well-known for their discretion, and visiting will save me the trouble of trying to pick someone up at a bar to quench my physical needs. Relationships are far too complicated when all I need is one night to get it out of my system.

I thought that's what I was here for until I looked up and saw *her*.

It's Ms. Kristoff all right, here in Octavio's, and she's wearing the shortest skirt I've ever seen in my life. A revealing corset top holds up her significant breasts, and her nipples are just barely visible. It's more skin than I've ever seen on her.

It's not just her body I find arresting. She's wearing dramatic dark makeup, with a black wig on top of it all. Gone is the blonde hair pulled back in a tight bun, and now she has dark hair cropped at her jawline. She's even colored her naturally light brows darker to match.

I notice everything when it comes to my assistant. I have her memorized, and these small shifts and changes have unnerved me beyond reason.

Glancing at the drink menu again, I'm so disconcerted that I pick something at random. "I'll have the Bombay Special."

Fuck. What am I saying? I don't want that. I just want a martini with two olives, but seeing Ms. Kristoff here, where I least expected her, has switched off my brain.

"Yes, sir," she says, smiling broadly. She's recovered from her surprise and now plays the flawless hostess. I admire how easily she slips into her nighttime persona.

How long has she worked here? How many other clients have touched her, maybe even been inside her? The thought sparks a searing flame as Ms. Kristoff—no, *Velvet*—turns around and departs with my drink order.

When she was simply my assistant, I could ignore the idea of what she did after hours. It was none of my business. In my mind, she vanished from existence the moment she left my sight. I tried, and succeeded, in never thinking about what her personal life might entail because it would only serve to infuriate me if I imagined her with a boyfriend or girlfriend. She wears no wedding ring, at least, so I always had that.

But here, knowing what the girls do as part of their work, I burn with the fire of an imploding sun. Now I can't help picturing her on top of one of those old men sitting nearby, moaning as she's filled, and I want to flip over the fucking table and then shatter it into matchsticks.

I could if I wanted, but I manage to stay in

my seat, stewing and steaming the entire time that Velvet is gone.

What a name to choose.

Am I not paying her enough? Why would she feel the need to take a second job? I've seen where she lives, and it's not as if it's out of her price range. She's in an apartment building on the lower end, one that should be perfectly affordable on her salary.

I puzzle over this while she's gone, but only a few minutes later, she reappears with the drink in her hand. Right. Not a martini. Still, I take it and sip in front of her, nodding my head in approval at the flavor. I will choke it down for her.

"May I sit with you?" she asks. I think she means sitting on my lap, and instantly, that's all I want. Yes, her ass pressing against my cock, her small body in my arms? I should leap at the chance. This is my opportunity to make even just a shred of my dream a reality.

"Yes," I say, pulling out the chair beside me. Confusion twists her face only briefly, before the practiced smile returns and Velvet gracefully places herself in the red cushions of the other chair.

What on earth do I say to her now? Instead

of trying to come up with something, I slide my drink across to her.

"If you would like some."

Velvet peers at me, then down at the drink before nodding agreeably. She takes a graceful, tiny sip, then puts the glass back on the table.

"Thank you," she says with that same bright smile I've never seen before. She doesn't smile like that at work, always focused on her job. "What brings you here tonight?"

Right. At least there's that—it's her role to make conversation.

"Needed some relaxation." If that's what I can call it. "A little downtime."

"You came to the right place." She shifts closer in her chair. "Why don't you give me your hand?"

I blink down at her, trying to figure out the rationale behind her question. But I come up blank, so I do as I'm told, extending my arm across the space between our armchairs to give her my hand. My green fingers look like sausages in her tiny, delicate, human ones.

And then, she starts to rub. Working her way around my palm at first, she digs in and then releases, massaging as she goes. It feels... exquisite, and also strangely painful. No one has ever massaged my hand before. She makes her way to my fingers next, squeezing each one from the base to the tip.

I wonder if she would handle my cock like that. Would she press down as she stroked it? Choke it as she sank her mouth down on it?

Fuck. I shouldn't be thinking like that, but it's impossible not to as I look into my assistant's face, her eyes shadowed with makeup, her lips a feral red. As to be expected, my dick responds under my slacks. It thickens and rises until I know Velvet can see it.

"Sir," she says in a silky voice, her gaze darting down to my waist and then back up to my face. "You know I can help you with that."

I practically choke on my drink. She's propositioning me, out in the open, with her own voice. Asking to touch me. Relieve me.

Against my will, my cock twitches inside my pants. But I can't. Not with my assistant. Not with Ms. Kristoff, who is off-limits to me.

I should request someone else, but I can't bring myself to do that, either.

Is this truly, perhaps, my opportunity? Could this be the moment I've been waiting so long for? I glance around the room, where no one is paying attention to us. Even if they did, all they would see is what they expect to see: a rich man in a suit with a beautiful, scantily dressed woman on his lap.

After a solid few moments of silence have passed, where Velvet patiently waits for my answer, I clear my throat.

"Please," I say, my voice coming out strained.

She nods with another smile, and climbs out of her chair, easily seating herself on my thigh. I utterly dwarf her like this, as if she is a child and I am Santa Claus.

Her touch. Her ass on my leg. Her hip against my belly. All the places we're connected turn white-hot.

Her hand snakes out, gently caressing the bulge that's formed under my slacks. She's gentle with it, skimming over the top, and I'm absolutely fucking electrified. I've never allowed myself anything, and here she is, caressing my dick with only two layers of clothing between us. I've been starving in the desert and now my mouth is buried in a trough of the world's sweetest water.

"Hmm," Velvet says, her voice low, tuned in a way I've never heard it before. "You seem trapped in there."

I don't even realize that my arm has extended around her, circling her back, as she reaches down to unfasten my belt. Next is the button and the zipper on my slacks, revealing my black boxer briefs. Normally, I am not self-conscious in the least about how I look, but I never expected the one on my lap at Octavio's to be Ms. Kristoff.

Damn, and I'm hard. Painfully hard as her hand strokes once again over the fabric like she's testing my shape underneath. My cock is ready to rip through my boxer briefs. I'm unable to move, simply watching in fascination as she hooks her thumb in the band and pulls it down, which lets me finally burst free.

Thank fuck I'm mostly hidden by the table.

Velvet gasps, and my arm curls tighter around her back. I hope she's not scared of it. It is a monster, the damned thing, already dribbling at the tip. Veins throb along the sides, leading up to the head that is a softer green than the rest of my skin.

Then, her petite human hand creeps up to the base, her fingers trying to wind around it. She can't even get close to connecting them on the other side.

"What was your name, sir?" she asks, giving it one gentle, testing stroke.

I almost forget my own name as she lifts her

hand partway up, then slides down to the root again. "Vincent Roth."

"Well, *Vincent*," she says in an alluring tone, "I can't wait to taste you."

She leans down, and I don't even try to stop her as she drags her tongue across the head of my cock. My hips surge against her, my body out of my own physical control. This is everything I've ever dreamed about all those long nights alone.

Well, not everything.

"Mm," Velvet hums, her lips vibrating against me. Fuck, that's good. "Yes, delicious." She strokes up with her hand and sinks me even deeper into her mouth, enveloping the whole head. I feel like I'm going crazy. I must be delirious, and this is my hallucination.

But I keep still, keep from showing any of this on my face, how deeply she affects me. How much I simply want to grab her head and push it down, or throw her onto the table and wrap her legs around my hips as I drive into her.

Because once I did, I wouldn't be able to stop.

CHAPTER
THREE

ROSETTE

wasn't lying. Mr. Roth does taste incredible. It's the earthiness of it, the way I can tell he isn't human just by his scent, his flavor. How there's a masculinity in it unlike anything I've come across, and let me tell you, I have sucked a lot of dick in Octavio's.

Mr. Roth—no, Vincent—doesn't give any indication of whether he's enjoying it, his face remaining impassive, those yellow eyes watching me. I decide to focus solely on pleasuring him, as is my job.

Of course I'm enjoying it, too. At long last, I

got to find out what was underneath those slacks. And good lord, is it incredible, fat and swollen and *throbbing*. It wants, this green thing. It hungers. I can sense it all the way to my toes that this would feel amazing inside me. Incredible.

Maybe I can convince him to go to one of the private rooms with me if I show him a good enough time. I'm going to get revenge on this orc for spending the last two years just staring.

I take him deeper into my mouth, pulling down his foreskin so I can swirl my tongue around that broad, monstrous cockhead. And still, Vincent hasn't moved. It doesn't even seem like his breathing has sped up.

That's all right. Sometimes it takes time to work a man to his finish. I go slow, simply enjoying, using both hands now to wrap around the base of him while I lick the tip like a lollipop. Then I sink him back in again, wrapping my lips around that wide girth, swallowing more and then applying suction as I pull him back out.

His right hand twitches.

Good. There we are. I go shallow again before trying for more, sucking him farther in, using my tongue to tantalize him. I'm stroking slightly faster with my hands, matching the speed of my mouth as I relax my throat. Then I slide him in as deep as I can take.

Vincent grunts, a quiet but carnal noise. Returning to the head, I tease it some more before I swallow him up again. And again. His hand drifts over to my head, and his fingers lightly land on my hair as I bury him into my throat, taking as much of his cock as space will allow. I lick along the underside as I go, and he's leaking even more. His hips jerk up, and I think he might be close.

Then, Vincent surges under me. His cock thickens in my mouth, and he grabs my hair in his hand. I squeeze the base of him as he comes, a low groan falling from his lips as he ejects. There's so much of it, and I swallow as fast as I can, but it's still spilling down my chin. It tastes incredible, and I never thought I'd say that about a man's—or an orc's—cum. But damn, I can't get enough.

When I let go, he's still surprisingly hard. I peer up to find Vincent's pupils are enormous, and he licks his lips like he just saw a delectable steak go past.

"Get on the table," he says in a low, dangerous voice.

Curious what he has planned, I do as he tells

me, getting off his lap and hiking myself up onto the edge of the table. It's secured to the floor, so I know it won't fall over on me, but it still unsettles me.

"Do you want to—" I begin, about to ask if he wants to go to one of the back rooms and lock the door instead of doing this on a table, when Vincent pulls back up his underwear, hiding his cock from me once more. Then he zips up his slacks, buttons them, and reattaches his belt.

"Oh," I say, disappointed.

"Never mind that." Vincent nods at me from his chair. "Spread your legs."

I don't ask questions. When the client tells you to do something like that, you do it. I make sure his drink is far enough away that I won't knock it over, then open my legs for him. I'm not wearing any underwear again, and I know he can easily see all of me.

"Good," Vincent says, reaching up to stroke one of his massive tusks. "Pull up your skirt."

Once again, I do as he says until I'm bare from the waist down. Vincent releases his tusk and scoots his chair closer. He hooks his hands under my ass and drags me forward on the table, spilling the drink but paying it no mind whatso-ever. Then he leans down until his head is be-tween my thighs.

He can't possibly be about to do what I think he's going to do. Then Vincent breathes on me, one hot gust of air, and I know he is.

First he simply licks, once, gliding over the outer lips of my sex. It's exploratory but not ten-tative. He licks again, firmly, his large tongue stimulating everything from my entrance up to my clit like he's tasting me, getting a sense of me.

I don't think anyone has eaten me out *here* before.

Vincent huffs as he leans in closer, like he's smelling me, and pushes my thighs apart even farther so he can fit his massive shoulders be-tween them. When he licks me again, it's more insistent, more focused right on my clit. His twin tusks are cool against my skin.

A powerful tremble spreads outward from the intense sensation on such a sensitive area. The massive orc doesn't relent, though, tracing his tongue over it in quick, successive strokes, until I'm gasping for air and my whole body is twitching under him.

Holy damn. He knows how to use his tongue.

"Mm," Vincent murmurs, and then I feel his fingers trace up the outside of my swollen labia. "Ready for me?"

I blink, not quite sure what he's asking, when he resumes licking even faster, even harder. And then one of those fingers gently dips inside me.

Oh. I understand now.

My body arches off the table as he slips that massive, thick finger through, pushing himself in up to the knuckle.

"Fuck," I whisper. I'm surprised at the slight stretch as I accommodate it. God, his hands are huge, aren't they?

Now, Vincent really gets into it. He pumps his finger slowly as his tongue whips me up higher and higher, making circles and then flicking side to side, caressing and rubbing in utterly delightful patterns. And that *finger*, the pad dragging along the inside of me with every thrust, draws each of my muscles and tendons tighter and tighter.

I'm definitely going to come like this. No question. And I never come at Octavio's.

I can't help a moan as Vincent hastens his pace, well and truly fucking me with his hand while he devours my clit. I'm shaking, completely out of control, not even realizing that I've grabbed the back of his head and buried my fingers in his hair, messing it up. But there's nothing I can do about it as I fall completely victim to him, writhing on the table, the two other men in the room staring unabashedly as Vincent destroys my pussy.

"Oh god," I chant, my hips moving of their own accord as I climb higher and higher. It's like the rainbow in the distance, but somehow, I'm getting closer to it, to the pot of gold at the end. Vincent's hand moves even faster as he continues his relentless assault, until I think that not only am I going to orgasm, but I might also burst open into a billion pieces that need to be swept up off the floor.

"There we go," Vincent says as I tighten around his finger, my thighs shaking on either side of his head. "Come for me, Velvet."

I wish it was my real name, not my stupid club name, but I'll take what I can get.

Then, I can't help it. My climax roars to the surface and sucks me under, delirious pleasure radiating out to every last corner of my body. Even my fingers and toes feel too tight as I release, and then I hear Vincent groan between my legs.

"Fuck," he mutters, his tongue laving over my painfully sensitive pussy. "You taste like heaven."

Wow. Never expected those words from my silent boss. But right now, he feels like so much more than that. He just gave me an absolutely world-altering orgasm, and I'm never, ever going to forget it.

When I finally manage to get my wits about me again, Vincent withdraws his finger and pops it into his mouth, sucking it clean from base to tip. I stare at him as he does it, baffled by this image of a mountain of an orc with everything he could want, with all the cash in the world at his disposal, eating me out on a table with a spilled drink next to us.

My eyes travel down his big body to his groin, where his cock is, once again, thick and hard under his slacks. He must be ready for round two.

And so am I. After that earth-shattering climax, I want nothing more than to feel him inside me. To see that big body without the suit covering it up. To have him on top of me, weighing me down, showing me what else he can do.

Unsteadily, I slip off the table and land on my feet, almost falling over. Vincent reaches out to steady me with a hand on my hip.

"Easy there," he says, gently pulling me closer to him. I let him bring me in, reveling in his touch after what an intimate thing we just did. I hardly ever feel this way after an experience at Octavio's, like I don't want to let my partner go.

I try to take Vincent's massive hand in mine, but the best I can do is wrap my fingers around his thumb. Then I lean down until my lips are at his ear.

"Would you like to go to a back room?" I whisper. "Where we can be alone?"

Most abruptly, Vincent shoots to his feet. I'm pushed back by the sudden movement and would have stumbled if it weren't for the table behind me.

When he stares at me, Vincent looks... formidable. Irate. His brows are drawn, his eyes narrowed, his tusks dragging down each side of his mouth in a deep frown. He steps away as if I'm poisonous.

Shit. What did I say?

"No," he says firmly, curling his hand into a fist at his side as if he's holding back from punching someone. "I will go pay my bill now."

I'm supposed to bring it to him, but he's already striding away, past the bouncer and out of the VIP lounge. I stare at his back, baffled and hurt, lost as to what I did wrong.

He pays at the front, then stalks out of Octavio's without a second look back.

CHAPTER
FOUR

VINCENT

Nothing in the world has ever tasted as good as Ms. Kristoff did, and as I stride quickly out of the club, I know I'll never forget her flavor as long as I live.

But I let it get away from me. I allowed my need to take over, and that was a mistake. She asked me to be alone with her, and I knew exactly what I would do to her if that happened. I would fuck her so fast and so hard, she would probably break apart.

Not with my assistant. One ought to never mix business with pleasure. Even at my position in the firm, such involvement is still a liability.

It's good I finally came to my senses when she suggested the back room, though perhaps I could have tempered my reaction.

But I'm angry. Now that I've tasted her delectable pussy, I'll want nothing else ever again. I've ruined myself for anyone else. I should never have partaken to begin with.

I stalk out of Octavio's and call up my car, which was waiting in a lot a few blocks over. When George arrives, I slide into the back seat and slam the door. George peers at me in the rearview mirror.

"I didn't expect you so soon," he says as we pull away from the curb.

"It wasn't what I had hoped."

No, it was far more. I could never have imagined I'd meet lovely little Ms. Kristoff dressed to kill, made up like a completely different person. Now my cock is thirsting, craving, still thick under my pants as I remember how sweet and succulent she was on my tongue.

George nods and falls silent as we drive back to my place. I have two apartments in the city, but I prefer my house, which is a bit farther out. It's a magnificent brownstone with a newly remodeled interior, vaulted ceilings and marble countertops, and big windows looking out over the river.

Once I'm home, I pour myself a martini and get started on dinner. My personal chef was over earlier today and left me a meal in the fridge, which I heat up to go with my drink.

But it tastes like ash in my mouth compared to the meal I had earlier. How am I going to face Ms. Kristoff tomorrow? I consider calling out sick, which I've never done, even when I had a nasty cold last year. But that would be cowardly, and I'd still have to see her again on Monday.

Unless I fire her.

I squash that thought when it flits through my mind. What happened tonight isn't Ms. Kristoff's fault, and it would be cruel of me to punish her for doing her after-hours job. Besides, where would I find another assistant like her? I've had half a dozen of them during my career, and none compared to her skill.

I need to go in tomorrow and pretend like nothing transpired between us. It will murder me, I think, not to touch her ever again when her skin was so smooth and soft under my hands, but I will just have to die and be reborn with new self-control.

With that certainty in mind, I clean up

dinner and head to bed. But the moment my eyes close, I remember Ms. Kristoff in my lap, her luscious mouth wrapped around my cock. She'd looked so good doing it, her skill un-matched. It usually takes more than a blowjob to make me come, but I'd unraveled in that wet, perfect mouth.

Now that I've drunk from her fountain once, I hunger for it. How would it look with my cock inside that delectable pussy, stretching it wide open for me? Yes, I would have to teach her. That would be a process. But once she could fit me, I would bring her to such heights of pleasure—

I need to knock some sense into myself. Pissed off, I get out of bed and head downstairs to my workout room. This is how a true orc deals with his problems: he fights them out. I don't have anyone to attack with a battle axe right now, though, so the weight room will have to do.

After a bit of warmup on the treadmill, I load weights onto my bar and deadlift it as many times as I can, until it feels like my legs are going to give out. Then I get back on the treadmill and run some more.

At last, it feels like I might be able to sleep. I

stumble back upstairs and fall into bed, but even as I lie there unconscious, she's in my dreams.

ROSETTE

Getting ready the next morning, I'm more terrified than I've ever been going to work.

What happened last night at Octavio's stays between us. That's my job, and I would never violate a client's trust. But the look on Mr. Roth's face as he left? The fury, the hatred?

I wonder what kind of disaster I'll be walking in on. I might even lose my job, now that he knows what I do outside of working for him.

Today, I stick to my daytime makeup—light concealer, a flourish of powder, some color on my eyelids and a few strokes of mascara. Nothing like what I had on last night at the club. I wear my best blouse and a matching skirt, this one longer than my usual. I'll be the perfect, demure personal assistant, exactly what Mr. Roth wants.

I'll give him no reason to fire me.

My hand is trembling just slightly as I stand outside my apartment. The car pulls up to the curb at nine on the dot, as it does every morning. I don't even dare look at Mr. Roth where he sits on the other side, pulling my feet inside, closing the door, and setting my purse into the seat back pocket like I always do. Then I keep my gaze straight forward as I scroll to my calendar app.

"Prospective client meeting at ten," I say. "Just enough time to get coffee and head to the other side of town."

I see from the corner of my eye as Mr. Roth nods, not speaking, same as he always does. The car pulls away as we head to the coffee shop. But as we drive in silence, it feels far more deafening than it ever did before. I'd grown so used to it, but now all I can think is that he's going to confront me about last night.

But he doesn't. I get our coffees as always and place them in the cupholders.

"Thank you," Mr. Roth murmurs, then picks up his coffee cup and brings it to his lips. I jerk my gaze away so I'm not staring at him.

He's never said that before, not in the two years I've worked for him.

My face heats as I drink my own coffee, trying to choke it down even though it's fresh and hot. Maybe he isn't mad at me after all.

When we reach the prospective client's office, I follow Mr. Roth inside. But this time, he holds the door open for me, and I stare at him quizzically before stepping through.

Inside the white foyer, Mr. Roth leads us down a hall to an office. Typically, I sit behind him and take notes, but as he sits down, my boss pulls out the chair next to him and gestures for me to sit there.

My jaw flexes, but I have no choice but to sit in the offered chair. I whip out my notebook, ready to take notes as the two start talking business.

On the way out, Mr. Roth holds the door open for me again, and I come so close to him as I pass that my ass almost touches his groin. He inhales sharply, but then I'm on the other side, striding down the hall. He follows along behind me, and I'm too scared to look back and see the expression on his face.

After he calls the car, we wait at the curb, and a gentle rain starts to fall. Mr. Roth puts one hand on my shoulder and guides me backward, under the overhang.

"Can't have the rain ruin your makeup," he says under his breath. Then he releases me, and we wait side by side for the car to arrive.

The rest of our day is much the same. At five, after Mr. Roth's last meeting, the car heads toward my apartment. I expect Mr. Roth to do something—anything—to give me an idea of what he's thinking, but as normal, the car stops outside my apartment and Mr. Roth is silent.

But when I put my hand on the door handle, his voice stops me.

"Thank you for your hard work today, Ms. Kristoff."

I turn around, and his yellow eyes are focused on me.

"Oh. Sure. It's... my job."

He nods, and then turns away, which I take as my sign to go.

That night, I luxuriate in the shower, touching my nipples as I think about Mr. Roth in the car today. Then my hand ventures south, and I brush over my clit as I remember his hand sliding up my thigh.

He was hard, too. I didn't miss that. I make him just as horny; I affect him just as much. So what will it take to convince him to make the next move?

I head to the club in my long overcoat, pondering as I ride the subway. This was not the day I expected to have after how we left things last night.

Once downstairs, I greet the other girls getting ready and tuck my belongings away into my locker. I have to shift into Velvet now, the after-hours girl, and try to shake off my weird day. Tonight, I'm sexy, available, and eager to please.

The club is packed, but every girl is working, so again, I don't get flagged down. When I reach the bar, though, Matt is waiting for me.

"He's back," he says conspiratorially.

"Who's back?"

"The gentleman from last night. Must have made an impression for him to come two nights in a row and inquire about you."

I freeze. No way. He's here. Vincent is here again, and he's been asking about me.

"Thanks for letting me know." I wave as I head off to the VIP room. Tonight I'm wearing a midriff-length, structured top with a high-waisted skirt, all of it black. The club is busier tonight, but I see right away when I step through the doorway that Mr. Roth is here again.

Vincent. He's sitting in the back by the wall at

a small table, alone. But then his nostrils flare, and his gaze jumps up to mine.

I don't know what to think as I weave my way toward Vincent's table. He's not smiling, but he's not frowning, either—just the blank expression I've come to expect from him as Mr. Roth.

"It's you," I say brightly, as if we left off last night and today at work never happened. "Didn't expect you to come back. Why did you leave last night?"

I guess Velvet will just put it all out there.

"I have my reasons." That's all he says in response. Then Vincent taps the drink menu. "Bombay Special, please."

Drink order in hand, I head back to the bar, trying to figure out how best to approach this. Matt makes the drink quickly, then I carry it back with me. What does my boss have planned for tonight?

"Sit with me," Vincent says when I return with the drink. Cautiously, I take a seat on his lap, and his arm loops around my back with an easy grace. He takes a sip, squinting as he does, as if he doesn't like the drink at all.

"Do you want me to return that?" I ask, but he just shakes his head.

I feel him growing thicker under my thighs. After a few moments, he pushes the drink aside.

"Get on the table," he says. His voice is steady and commanding. Surprised, I do as I'm told, pushing the drink out of the way again so I can sit on the edge. A few heads in the room turn to look at us, but most everyone else is occupied with a conversation or with one of the girls working the floor.

Vincent grunts low in his throat. "Pull your skirt up."

What? He can't possibly mean that he wants to do that again. Still, I do as the client says, hiking my skirt up so I'm bare from the hips down.

Vincent's eyes slide down between my legs, and he wets his lips. Again, he pushes my thighs wide apart so he can wedge himself between them, then he bends down and licks me from ass to clit.

Oh, fuck. I'm toast.

CHAPTER
FIVE

ROSETTE

This is not at all how I expected my night to go, with Vincent's hands cupped under my butt as he fucks me with his tongue. This time, he jams it inside me as if trying to lick up as much as possible, curling it to rub the tip along my channel. I'm trembling as he withdraws it and returns to circling and lapping my clit, then sucking on it like a nipple.

Damn, I'm already close, and he's only just started playing with me. He works me even more expertly than last night, until I'm shaking and trembling and pushing the drink farther away so it doesn't spill.

And then, Vincent uses his finger. That bonus pressure, sliding in and pushing me open, nearly does me in. God, how does he send me to the brink so easily, like I'm his puppet? Soon I'm moaning, writhing on the table, completely oblivious to everything around us.

That's when he uses a *second* finger. It pushes in, but together they're so broad that I have to spread even wider to accommodate. The stretch is glorious, even if intense, and my hips arch off the table.

"Mm," Vincent hums, the first sound I've heard him make. "This pussy is delicious."

All I can do is answer with a cry when he curls his fingers and pushes them in deeper, seeking something. Then he brushes over a supremely sensitive spot, and I'm so near the edge that I can see the rocks far down below.

"Vincent," I moan, clutching his head, seeking anything I can grab. Saying his name only seems to embolden him, and he licks even faster, pumping his hand in perfect rhythm, and I'm a goddamned goner.

It explodes out of me like a volcano erupting. I sense it when my body clamps down tight around his hand, and my thighs squeeze together of their own accord. I'm like a star, expanding and then bursting, and Vincent groans as I writhe and shake.

"Yes, come all over me," he says, his voice thick and full of desire.

And then, without warning, he starts licking again.

Oh fuck. I try to wriggle away, my clit so sensitive I think it might erupt in flames, but Vincent stops me, keeping my hips rooted to the table.

"No," he growls low in his throat. "Stay where I put you."

I whimper as he renews his attack, my entire body tensing and shivering while he resumes stroking with his fingers. I'm already so high on my orgasm that this sends me catapulting even higher, and a new, blistering pressure is building deep in my belly. Vincent devours me more vigorously, his hand making wet noises as it slicks in and out, and I'm clutching his head, the only buoy I have in this storm.

"Ah!" I've completely forgotten where we are, what's around us, as my hips buck on the table. "Vincent, please!"

He grunts, never releasing me. It isn't a few seconds before I'm launching skyward again, moaning almost miserably as another massive climax is yanked out of me, and much to my surprise, I start to *pee*.

"Fuck!" I try to pull away, but Vincent is holding me tight. He lets out a feverish moan of his own as I leak all over him, and I'm whimpering and fighting as he keeps me from escaping. My entire body flushes with humiliation as, at last, he pulls his fingers free of my pussy.

"I'm so sorry," I say as I sit up on the table, horrified at myself. I try to climb off so I can go clean up. "I don't know what happened, I didn't mean to—"

"Stop."

Vincent's voice is hard as stone. I do as he says, remaining exactly where I am. He looks up at me then, running his hands down my thighs.

"Was that new for you?"

I nod, covering my face with my hands. "I've never done that before, I promise, again, I'm so—"

"Velvet." He grabs my chin in his hand, forcing me to stare him in the eyes. "That was natural. It means I did such a good job that I made you gush all over my face."

I suck in a calming breath to still my racing heart. Then I realize that yet again, we've knocked over his drink. I hastily climb off the table, pulling my skirt down, and pick up the glass. "Would you like another?"

Vincent's eyes roll over me, like he's judging me. I never fidget, but right now, I shift from foot to foot while I wait for his answer.

"All right."

I take off to get his drink, trying to set my mind straight again after the mind-blowing orgasm I just had. No, not just one—two of them in a row. Damn. And he's the one paying *me?*

At the bar top, other girls are waiting for their customers' orders, and Bunny shoots me a look.

"Who's that guy who keeps coming in and eating you out?" she asks. "Trade with me sometime. I wouldn't mind at all."

I shake my head, unable to put it into words. During the day, he's my boss. But here, at night, he's someone else. Someone who wants to consume me from the inside out.

VINCENT

Who knows what I'm doing here a second time. I couldn't get Velvet out of my head. Then, she exploded all over my face, and fuck, that was so hot I almost went off in my own slacks. Now she's on her way back, her perfect hips swaying as she carries a fresh martini glass in my direction.

A martini glass. With two olives in it.

She approaches and sets it on the table, then slides into the bench seat beside me. Her hands are threaded together in her lap, awaiting my judgment.

I don't say out loud that this isn't what I ordered. It's what she knows I really wanted.

Sipping my drink, I loop my arm around her, pulling her in close against my side. I won't ask anything else of her tonight, not after what we just did. She tries to reach over and touch my cock, but I stop her hand and return it to my thigh.

She understands the message and doesn't try again.

"What do you do for work?" Velvet asks at length, her customer service smile still on.

"Finance. Investments." I reach into my pocket for a cigar, then pull it out and cut off the tip. "Nothing exciting."

"Sounds exciting to me." She picks up my

lighter and flicks it, bringing the flame to the tip of my cigar. I inhale until it lights.

"It's money. Just money and more money. What do you do? With your time off?"

Her brows lift like no one's ever asked her this question before, and maybe they haven't.

After a moment, she answers. "Mostly self-care. Working out. Cleaning my house. Doing laundry. Sometimes I go to the bar with my friends." She thinks for a time. "Said friends are single-serving friends, though. Good for a night out on the town, but not much else. When I need a heart-to-heart, I call up my friend from middle school who still lives back across the country. It's been a while since I phoned her, though. Maybe it's time."

That's much more than I expected to receive. So she lacks more meaningful connections in the city. I can't say I have much in the way of close friends, either. It's never been important to me. I make connections in business, and those are my "friendships," if I could ever call them that.

"And what do you do outside of work?" Velvet asks me.

"Nothing special. I stay late at the office or work at home. Then I lift. I can't say I do laundry or cook, though." I smirk. "I have people who do that for me."

She answers with a mischievous grin of her own. "That sounds nice. I'd love to never have to do laundry again."

"I suppose I play some Gekaran," I say after a moment of silence.

"What's that?"

"An orcish game, much like your solitaire. It's meant to be played alone, always trying to be better at solving the puzzle than the time before."

I eat one of my olives, then tip back more of my martini. It's easy talking with her, this *Velvet*. She is curious and forward, eager and pleasant. I wonder how much of her personality she truly shares with Ms. Kristoff, and how much is the show she puts on working at Octavio's.

"How did you end up in finance?" Velvet asks, her hand stroking my chest in a way that's supremely comforting. "You don't run across many orcs in the city."

"I grew up in an orc clan in the mountains. But I knew that kind of isolated life wasn't for me, so I came to the city instead. Worked my way up here."

Her brows lift. "Humble beginnings."

We talk for another hour, perhaps two—I'm not entirely sure. But the longer I sit beside Velvet, breathing in the musky scent of her perfume, the harder it is not to simply grab her by the hand and drag her off to one of the private rooms in the back.

Eventually, I know it's time for me to go or I won't have as much control over what I do next. The alcohol has gone to my brain. I'm an orc, and orcs conquer. We take what is ours, leaving no prisoners. And what I want now more than anything is *her*. Already, my arm is around her middle, my hands cupping her perfect breasts. When did that happen? She's nearly in my lap, and surely she can feel how eager I am, how desperately my cock longs to be free and find its way inside her.

"I must go." I hastily extract myself, setting Velvet down on the seat before I rise to my feet. She blinks up at me, surprised.

"It's still early." She is about to extend a hand to me when she must see the fire in my eyes, because she withdraws it.

"I go to bed early." I fish out my cash and put it on the table. "Thank you for your company tonight, Velvet."

She nods, unsure. "Of course, Vincent. I'm here every Thursday, Friday, and Saturday night."

So I could come and see her tomorrow? It's painfully alluring, but I have an engagement with a congressman.

"Thank you." I take her hand and bring it to my lips, pressing them to the soft skin on the back. "I will see you again soon."

Even when I am outside in the cool evening air, though, I can't slow the rapid beating of my heart.

CHAPTER
SIX

VINCENT

Tasting Velvet has unlocked something in me, and making her gush all over my face only emboldened me. I've always known that she likes my attention, that she wants me to cross the line between us, but until now, I've held myself back.

She is my employee, and I'm her boss. It's a human resources disaster. But after having her, I don't know that I can maintain that boundary any longer.

On Sunday, I try to mellow myself with a game. Pondering my next move, I tap my Gekaran token against the table. It has five marks on it arranged in a pattern. Where it goes on the board depends on the other numbered tokens. I do some quick calculations in my head, then place the token where it should go.

I score across three rows and add it to my tally.

Picking up my next token, I ponder what this attraction to Ms. Kristoff means. There is something *more* to her, something that demands exploring, something that calls to me in a voice that only I can hear.

I can't help myself. She is too delicious, too savory a morsel for me to leave alone. Having her as Velvet isn't enough, not when she stretches the confines of her blouses all day, when her perfect ass moves under her work skirts with a slight bounce. I can't stay away.

I know it's dangerous ground we're walking, but as foolish as it is, my will is weaker than my hunger.

This one is a seven. A bit harder to find a home for.

It's time, I believe, to stop fighting my desire. I have no need to mate, but I do have an aching for Ms. Kristoff. And I think she feels that ache for me, too.

There. I see the perfect spot for my seven

and place it. I didn't get a row bonus this time, but I will in a few more moves. This is one of my best games yet.

But tomorrow will be even better.

ROSETTE

When Vincent strides out the door, I'm disappointed. He truly opened up to me as Mr. Roth never has, telling me where he came from, how he ended up here. I am not surprised to find he does little with his spare time outside of work.

He's all I can think about the rest of the night, and he's in my thoughts even as I fall asleep.

The next day is no better. I spend my day wondering if Mr. Roth will come back to the club again that night. I'd been disappointed when he didn't let me touch his cock. I wonder if I did a poor job last time.

I take it easy until it's time for work. Then I put on my best outfit, a red velvet dress with a short skirt and matching red garters. But hours pass, and Mr. Roth never appears. I spend my time with other clients, though my eyes are always on the door, watching to see if he arrives.

At last, the night comes to an end. No one asked me to go to the back room, which I'm strangely grateful for. Usually I enjoy it, but today, I'm only interested in one orc.

I spend my Sunday catching up on chores and getting my nails done, then go out to happy hour with my friends. I don't tell any of them what's going on at work, or how Mr. Roth has been coming to Octavio's. They all know what I do, but I rarely divulge details, so none of them ask for more.

But it's vapid talk, and I'm caught up in wondering what Monday holds.

Soon, it's time to see Mr. Roth again. I wait with nervous energy at the curb for the car to arrive, just as it does every morning. What will he do today?

When it pulls up, he is exactly where I expect. He does, however, greet me good morning, and thanks me again when I get him his coffee.

We head to a client meeting at a breakfast location. Once more, Mr. Roth seats me beside him. During the conversation, though, some-thing gently brushes my thigh.

It's Mr. Roth's hand, hidden under the table.

I can't believe it. He's *touching* me, on the job. A shiver spreads through my entire body, but I try to keep my mind on what they're discussing. We're getting to the sensitive details now, before we lock in the deal, and I need to be accurate and precise in jotting them down.

The hand never leaves, nearly stealing my attention, and it's wonderfully warm through the fabric of my skirt.

The rest of the day passes the same way, his hand sneaking touches here and there. I return them, being so bold as to take his thumb during a meeting and push his fingers down toward my inner thigh. Mr. Roth stiffens all over, but his mouth manages to pick up the conversation going on over the desk like nothing happened underneath it.

It's dangerous, I know. If anyone saw us—if anyone here in the office found out... we'd be toast. But at last, Mr. Roth has crossed the line.

And I'm waiting for him on the other side.

When we head to my apartment that evening, Mr. Roth rolls up the tinted glass between us and George. Then he turns to me, his beastly body looming.

"Ms. Kristoff." He glares down at me with those yellow eyes, pupils big and black. "You were... a very bad girl today."

I suck in a breath as his hand slides over the leather seat to my thigh. There he squeezes, his pupils growing even larger.

"I'm sorry," I say, twitching as his hand slides down to my knee, where my skirt ends. I'm not really sorry, though.

"Are you?" His lip tweaks up on one side, as if all this is amusing him greatly. It's probably the most I've ever seen him smile. "I don't think you are."

His hand ducks under the skirt and then slides up the inside, revealing my thigh. My breath speeds up as he exposes me like this in the car.

"You like it when I touch you." He doesn't say it like a question. "What kind of woman likes to be touched by her boss?"

"Me," I say immediately, wanting him to go even higher. I'm so warm between the legs, and I know he can help quench my thirst. "A woman like me."

Mr. Roth chuckles dryly. His hand travels up

even farther, coasting toward the crux of my legs where I'm probably already getting my underwear damp. But then, the car stops, and over the speaker George says, "We are at Ms. Kristoff's residence."

Mr. Roth withdraws his hand and smooths my skirt back down. Then he gestures for me to get out of the car, so I do, stepping out onto the street. He nods at me as I close it, and then the car drives away.

What the fuck just happened?

The next morning, I'm surprised when I open the car door and Mr. Roth isn't there at all.

No, sitting on his seat is a little black box with a red bow tied around it.

"For you," George says over the seat. Then he rolls up the privacy window so I'm completely alone.

Perplexed, I take the box and untie the ribbon, then open it. It looks like perhaps a very large jewelry box, so I'm expecting to find some sort of necklace inside.

Instead, though, I'm greeted by a series of large purple phallic objects. The smallest one is a tad more slender than my vibrator at home, while the largest is... *large*. Very large.

A small note sits underneath them. I take it out, and it's printed in embossed gold letters.

Ms. Kristoff,

Should you be interested, please use these. There is an instruction sheet below this note that will assist you.

If you are not interested, simply leave the box in the car.

You have the day off today.

Best,

Vincent Roth

I stare at the note, realizing we still haven't left my curb yet. Setting it aside, I see the mentioned instruction sheet and start reading.

It's a dilator set, intended to encourage pelvic floor relaxation and stretch open the vaginal tissue. The sheet describes how the user should start small and work their way up.

Again, I gape down at the largest phallus. There's no way that would fit inside me, right? It's a beastly thing, immense and intimidating.

There's only one possible implication for this gift: Mr. Roth wants to have sex. And the biggest dilator in the set is close to the size of his dick.

Holy shit. I held it, I licked it, but seeing it

like this out in the open... I'm not sure I can take that *there*.

I knock on the window, and George rolls it down.

"I guess I'm leaving," I tell him.

He nods. "I will pick you up tomorrow at the usual time."

I wonder if he has any idea about the gift I was just given, but Mr. Roth is very private, so I doubt it.

Nodding absently, I take the box with me as I get out of the car. When I shut the door, it pulls away, and I'm strangely disappointed. I thought I would get to see Mr. Roth today, but I suppose he has more important things he wants me to do.

Carrying the box, I head inside my apartment. I don't think I've ever been home on a weekday like this, not since I had the flu a year ago. It all feels surreal with morning light streaming in the windows and cars honking as they go by.

I have a job today, though. And I very, very much want Mr. Roth to fuck me, so I had better do it.

I manage to get to the third dilator in the set before I can't take any more. There's no way he's as big as the biggest one, right? I think back to the first time Mr. Roth came into Octavio's, and I couldn't even fit my hand around him. He filled my mouth as full as it could be.

God, maybe it really is true to size. Is my body even capable of taking that?

After grabbing lunch at the lot of food carts, I puzzle over the next two dilators. Maybe if I really lube it up, it'll work. But as hard as I try, I'm just not ready yet.

Damn. How long is this going to take?

Eventually, I work up the courage to text Mr. Roth. I only have his business phone, but I have a feeling he uses it as his personal one, too. I don't think he has much separation between his professional and personal lives.

I got to the third one.

I don't get an answer right away, but I didn't expect one. He's probably busy with meetings, and I wonder how he's faring without me there to take notes.

Then, half an hour later, the reply comes.

Good. You have tomorrow
off, too.

I gape down at my phone. He can't be serious. I don't need the time off, and I feel idle not
being at work when I usually am.

You don't need me?

I need you very much. Which is
why you have the day off. Paid.

Oh. I see.

I understand.

There are no further messages after that, not
that I need one. I know now what he expects me
to do, and I'll do it if it means I get what I want.

CHAPTER
SEVEN

ROSETTE

By the end of the second day, I'm bored out of my skull, but I managed to make the largest of the dilators fit. Even though it was a stretch, I made sure to use it plenty, rubbing my clit at the same time that I fucked myself with it—all while imagining it was Mr. Roth inside me, instead.

I might have orgasmed quite a few times.

The following day, I'm anxious and excited for what he has in store for me. I wait on the curb shifting from foot to foot, trying not to chew my cuticles. I never have nerves like this, not even the time I entertained an ambassador at Octavio's.

Then the car pulls up with its tinted windows, so I won't know until I open the door whether Mr. Roth is there or not. I take a steadying breath as I pull on the handle, and inside, he sits in his usual seat. I slide in, put my purse in the pocket, then close the door behind me.

As is typical, Mr. Roth says nothing. He doesn't even look at me as I put on my seatbelt and George drives off. Taking out my phone, I look at his calendar for the day.

It's a busy one. First, he has a meeting with a client at the office, and then a one-on-one with the CEO. After that, we're visiting two sites, and one of them is a good long way out of town.

I'd almost expected to see a meeting with me on the schedule, but there isn't one.

We head to the main building first, and Mr. Roth holds the front doors open for me as we go inside. On my way past, his hand brushes my ass —just a tiny breath of contact, but one that electrifies me.

We wait in the elevator silently until we reach the fifth floor, then step off. Mr. Roth waves a hand for me to walk in front of him, so I do, though I used to always trail behind him wherever we went.

Once we're inside his office, I expect him to bend me over the desk, but instead he sits down in his chair and boots up his computer. I find my usual seat at my own desk in the back of the office, away from the windows.

Abruptly, Mr. Roth stands up again. He walks over to my desk, his leather dress shoes clicking on the floor, and stops in front of it. Then, without warning, he bends forward and *picks it up*. Carrying it like little more than a matchstick, he relocates the desk—leaving me still sitting in my chair—closer to his own, so they form an L shape. Then he sets it down and gestures to me.

"Come, sit."

I get out of my chair and wheel it over, utterly perplexed. I've always sat in the back, just the note-taker. But now he wants me closer?

Sitting once more, I tuck myself in. Mr. Roth nods, pleased, and returns to his seat. Only a few minutes of silence later, the client arrives.

I take thorough notes of the conversation, as I always do. Things get a bit heated, but Mr. Roth keeps his cool as he tells the client he won't be meeting their offer. He wants a cheaper buy-in, which upsets the man immensely, but Mr.

Roth simply sits with his arms crossed while the human rages about how much Mr. Roth is undervaluing their company.

With that order of business finished, we have thirty-five minutes until Mr. Roth's appointment with the CEO. She's intimidating, but he handles her with the same indifferent aplomb as he does anyone else.

Mr. Roth rises, probably to get water from the dispenser, but instead he walks past it. He grabs a string hanging from the ceiling and pulls, which releases a curtain I didn't even know was there. It drops down, covering the glass wall. He repeats this on the adjoining wall, which covers the door, too. Now we're hidden from the rest of the office, with only the windows left that look out over the city.

"On my desk," Mr. Roth says suddenly, startling me. His yellow eyes are intense, burning. I do as I'm told, scrambling out of my chair and approaching his wide mahogany desk. He follows me, reaching around me to shove his computer monitor and tin full of pens off to one side, then I hop up so I'm sitting on the edge.

Mr. Roth looms over me, a beast, a giant. His shoulders are so broad that I'm surprised he can fit through most doorways. No wonder his cock is the size of that dilator.

First, he slides up my skirt until I'm exposed to the base of my thighs.

"Pull down your tights," he says, voice unchanged.

I nod, pulling the skirt up higher so I can reach the band. I pull them down, wriggling a bit on the desk to get them out from under my butt.

"Underwear, too."

Swallowing, I do it, until my tights and my lacy red underwear are both at my knees. Mr. Roth uses one big, meaty hand to push my thighs apart, and he wets his lips with his tongue the way he did at Octavio's. He tugs upward on his slacks and then, to my surprise, gets into a kneeling position. He's still huge like this, his broad body now between my spread knees.

I know what he's going to do. Right here, in his office, he's going to eat me out again.

Not a second later, he leans in and licks, uttering an almost silent groan as he does.

"This delicious fucking pussy," he mutters, more to himself than to me. Then he buries his face in it, smothering me with his tongue, his lips. I know I need to keep quiet with the receptionist not thirty feet from Mr. Roth's door, but it startles me so much I almost whimper.

Before I know it, two big fingers are pushing inside me. It's much, much easier to take them this time, and my boss lets out a long, satisfied breath.

"You used them." It's not a question. "Good."

I feel light as air when he says it. He goes to town sucking on my clit, making figure eights around it, whirling me up while his fingers steadily pump in and out. It's only a few seconds of this before I'm spiraling, trying to find something on the desk to grab onto while he rocks my world.

Abruptly, he stops. When I peer down at Mr. Roth, his wide mouth is wet with me, and his severe tusks are pulled down in a frown. I realize now that it's perhaps not what I thought it was —an expression of distaste—so much as how he looks when he's at his most intense and focused.

"Ms. Kristoff." He rises to his feet again, and his hand finds its way down to his belt, which he easily unbuckles. Next goes the button on his slacks, then the zipper. He tugs down his pants and underwear until his cock bursts out like an animal freed from its prison.

It is most certainly as big as the dilator, green

and throbbing, with veins spidering up the thick sides.

"Yes?" I ask, my voice coming out much more mousy than I expected.

"I want you to bend over the desk." He strokes himself once, from root to tip, and pre-cum drips down from the head. "Now."

VINCENT

Finally. I didn't have to think twice for my cock to get rock hard while I slurped up Ms. Kristoff's incredible cunt. Now she's over my desk, her pale, rounded ass in the air while she glistens and drips. The lips of her pussy are swollen and pink, as aroused as she is.

Ideal.

I approach her slowly, enjoying the sight of her body rising and falling with her labored breaths. I'm close enough now that I can lift my cock, pull back my foreskin, and rub the bare head over her clit. Ms. Kristoff lets out a gasp, and the interior petals of her pussy flex.

I can't wait to find out how she feels there.

Keeping my breathing even and steady, I drag

my head up and down, smearing my pre-cum all over her. Once she's wet with me, I notch myself right at the juncture of her thighs, below the tiny bud of her asshole. I know she trained, and Ms. Kristoff is diligent if anything, but I still worry that it won't work. That I won't fit inside her, and I'll never get to know the truth.

Fucking human women is always a challenge. I haven't attempted it in almost a decade, but here I am, because no one has ever called to me, beckoned me, the way Ms. Kristoff has.

I push in slightly, testing her opening to see how soft she is for me. The head of my cock squeezes through, and Ms. Kristoff lets out a muffled moan. It's quiet, quiet enough that the receptionist won't hear it.

Good. I hope she can keep it that way.

I pull back slightly and test it again, pushing in deeper, making sure she can take me. I'm widest about halfway down, and that will be the true test.

She's tight, so goddamned tight that I'm already gritting my teeth, my balls shivering with anticipation. She's juicy and soft inside, waiting to accept me, and I can't help sliding into her even farther. Her hips buck, and she covers her mouth with one hand.

Even better.

I grip her ass and watch, mesmerized, as her pussy spreads for me, and she squeezes me with every one of her labored breaths. I pull back again, trying to temper myself, doing everything in my power not to simply bury myself inside her in one powerful thrust.

"Mr. Roth," whimpers Ms. Kristoff. "Please, I want—"

She cuts herself off, and I pause, wondering what she was going to say.

"What do you want, Ms. Kristoff?" I ask, shallowly teasing her.

"I want *you*." She's whispering, but it's forceful. "Fuck me, please."

I narrow my eyes. I had planned how this was going to go, how I was going to work her up slowly over the next half hour, ratcheting her pleasure higher and higher until she burst open for me like a ripe fruit. But if she's going to beg me like that...

On my next thrust, I push in deeper, all the way up to the halfway point. Ms. Kristoff buckles forward, her arm spreading out across the desk so she clacks my keyboard. She moans into her hand as I withdraw, then slam myself in again, even farther.

She's fucking perfect, opening for me like a flower, her body giving to me so easily. The true orc in me rises to the surface, entranced by this delectable offering, ready to bury my seed in her and watch her get fat with my child.

I'm caught off-guard by that thought. She's human, so I can't impregnate her, but the fantasy returns again, fiercer. Put all my cum inside her. Get it in deep, so it goes where it's supposed to go.

My spine tingles, the warning signs of my climax already making themselves known. Fuck. I was going to draw this out for far longer, but her asking me to take her roughly has sped up the timeline.

I'm going to fuck this woman until she wishes she could scream.

CHAPTER
EIGHT

ROSETTE

Oh, is it a chore to keep my mouth shut, to hold anything in that isn't a small whimper or a hoarse moan. Mr. Roth feels so absolutely blissful that I just want my scream to fill up this whole office. He picks up his pace, pressing himself in deeper with each thrust, but it's still not enough.

I didn't just learn to take the diameter, but also the length of the dilator. I had a feeling that if Mr. Roth was big, then he would probably be long, too. That was harder to learn to take, but I managed to fit almost all of it in by the end of the day yesterday.

In real life, Mr. Roth feels so, so much better —smooth and soft, and yet hard in the best of ways. The way he digs his fingers into my ass with every thrust, even though he emits no noise at all, I can tell that he's keeping a tight hold on himself. He *wants* to fuck me ragged but is exercising patience.

He doesn't need to.

"More," I whisper, pushing my hips back at the same time that he shoves himself in. He's wider here, and my body struggles to take it. But he manages, and then I'm so fucking *full* that I bite my lip and cover my mouth both so the sound of my cry can't escape.

Now, Mr. Roth is panting as he reels back and then plunges in, sinking even more of that impossible beast inside me. I feel his balls against my clit, and he must be almost fully sheathed.

"Yes!" I try not to say it too loud, but I want him to know how good he feels.

"Is that where you like it?" Mr. Roth leans down over me, settling one hand on the desk next to my head as he sinks into me again. "Right there, Ms. Kristoff?"

Saying my name that way, my business name

while he's buried up to the hilt inside me, nearly makes me snap.

"Right there," I answer, and with a grunt, Mr. Roth speeds up even more, slamming into me at the exact same angle, giving me everything I need with each pump of his powerful hips. He's fucking me harder now, the desk itself moving with every thrust as he braces against it. I'll be shocked if the receptionist doesn't hear the wood feet dragging on the floor as he shunts forward again.

"Damn," he mutters under his breath, gripping me tighter in his hand as he shoves in deep, then yanks it back. Though he's moving in a punishing, brutal rhythm, he's also careful and intentional, too—making sure to find my spot with every thrust and attacking it relentlessly. This is exactly how I like it, rough and carnal and pushing all my buttons at once.

"What a bad girl," Mr. Roth growls into my ear as he spreads my legs even farther apart, nearly tearing my underwear at my ankles. "Fucking her boss in the middle of the workday."

I moan into my hand. I am bad, and damn, it feels good. It's everything I've wanted since I started working here.

"I didn't know my assistant liked it rough." He chuckles as if he isn't in the middle of fucking me. "But I should have expected it. Showing me your tits, bending over to give me a good look at your ass."

I press my lips into my palm, trying not to make a sound, but he's taking me with such dastardly precision, stimulating everything that begs to be stimulated, that I'm very close to breaking apart.

"You like me looking at you, don't you?" Mr. Roth's hand snakes down between us, and he slows for just a moment as his finger finds my clit. "You like making me hard for you?"

Oh, god. He's going to touch me at the same time.

"Now you get to find out where that takes you, Ms. Kristoff. What a slut like you deserves."

He fucks me harder, his finger rubbing back and forth over my clit, and there's no way I'm going to survive this. Not a chance, not while he calls me such filthy things.

"Mr. Roth," I whine, keeping my voice as quiet as I possibly can while he's filling me so full I might pop. "I'm going to come. I'm—I'm—"

He snarls like an animal, rubbing me harshly as he plunders me. "Good. Let go."

So, on command, I do. I bite my palm as it roars through me, an explosive tidal wave of pure pleasure, whirling me around like Dorothy caught in a tornado. I mutter expletives as it consumes me, tightening every muscle, clamping down hard around Mr. Roth's delicious cock.

"Squeeze me, Ms. Kristoff, like the hungry woman you are," he says as he slams into me again, shoving his way through all my clenching muscles. "And I'm going to give you everything."

That's when I sense him swelling, thickening, pushing me even wider for him all while I clamp down. I moan helplessly as he fully sinks in, spreading my edges as far as they'll go, and he lets out a low groan as he erupts inside me. There's so much of it that immediately, I feel it spilling out, wet droplets sliding down my bare thighs.

Both of us are breathing hard, and my heart is beating a frantic staccato inside my chest. Mr. Roth releases his grip on me and, more gently than I thought he was capable of, he pulls his cock free. Even more of his cum gushes down, probably getting all over my underwear.

I think that's going to be it, that Mr. Roth is done with me, when he leans over me and presses his nose into my hair. He breathes in deep as his hand skims across my ass softly.

When he pulls back, I glance over my shoulder to see him tucking his spent cock back into his boxers, then he zips up his fly and buttons his slacks. I'm shivering all over and much less graceful as I try to stand up. When I turn around, Mr. Roth has a wad of tissue in his hand. He passes it to me, and I do my best to clean up while he returns to his seat at the desk.

I inspect my ruined underwear. Unfortunately, I have no choice but to put them back on. So I do, and my ruined tights, too.

"Mm." Mr. Roth inhales deeply. "You're going to smell like my cum all day."

My face and neck turn hot, red hot, thinking about how much I must stink of sex right now. I need to go clean off.

"Don't even think about it." My head snaps up when he says it. "You can go to the bathroom, but you must come right back without cleaning it up."

I do very much need to pee, so I nod quickly and dart from the office. In the bathroom, I try to pay attention to his instructions, not wiping up the cum dripping down my thigh even though I desperately want to.

When I head back to his office, I take a peek at the receptionist's face, but she's simply working and ignoring me. Thank god.

All the curtains have been raised again, and Mr. Roth sits at his desk, typing. He doesn't look up when I enter, so I sit and start going through my notes while we wait for the meeting.

With the CEO. Right after *that*.

He pauses, sniffs the air, and gives me an approving nod.

VINCENT

My sweet little assistant smells like *me*. That's my cum all over her, painting her thighs, her delectable cunt. Other humans won't be able to pick up the scent, but if any other orc comes within even fifty yards of her, they'll know.

She's mine.

That probably won't happen, being as this is the finance sector and orcs still mostly keep to our old clan homes in the mountains, but you never know. Perhaps it's foolish, but I can't seem to stop the part of me that's desperate to claim her, to mark her.

After our meeting with the CEO, we head out to visit two potential sites. At our second site, though, an ogre pauses and sniffs the air. I glare daggers, putting my body between him and Ms. Kristoff, and his brows rise high on his forehead. Then he nods and walks off, without any words passing between us.

A shiver crawls up my spine, but I can't tell if it's apprehension or excitement. Maybe both. Afterward, Ms. Kristoff gives me an odd look, like she's trying to suss out what just happened.

But she doesn't need any funny ideas in her head about what this means, what we are. I'm her boss. She's my employee. That will not change until I get this out of my system and I can finally move on.

At last, we're on our way back to the city, heading to Ms. Kristoff's apartment to drop her off. I roll up the tinted privacy window between us and George, and her big eyes get even bigger.

"We have fifteen minutes," I tell her as I unbutton my slacks, then slide down the zipper. I've been on the edge of an erection ever since we fucked in my office, and now that we're alone, it's ready to be inside her again, to show her pleasure again, to make her come all over me.

"Oh." She blinks down at my cock, and then a smirk turns up her lip.

"You've been a bad girl today," I growl. "Walking around all covered in my cum."

She nods. "Drenched in it, Mr. Roth."

Her saying my name sends a ripple of anticipation into my balls. I nod to her hips, and understanding what I desire, Ms. Kristoff peels down her underwear and hose—which I notice have a rip up the inside of the thigh. Very good.

She takes them all the way off her feet, then navigates her way over the car seat and into my lap. There we are. My cock is wedged neatly between her thighs, the shaft skating along her pussy, already wet for me. To make sure she's ready, I reach down between us and rub her clit, making her gasp and shake. Her arms weave around my neck, and I'm surprised to find her face so close to mine. I turn my head so we are not tempted to kiss, redirecting my attention to the way her marvelous breasts press at the confines of her blouse.

I can't kiss her. That's not what this is. This is a physical relief, nothing else.

When it seems like Ms. Kristoff is good and ready for me, I lift her up by the ass with one hand, taking on her weight as I fist my cock and guide it in. My assistant gasps as I slide inside her in one smooth motion, as stretched and warmed up as she was by our escapade earlier today. I find my seat deep down, settling into the warm confines of her cunt.

Damn, she is perfect. Beyond the realm of possibility. Being inside her is an out-of-body experience, as is looking down into her warm hazel eyes. I use both hands now to lift her, reeling my hips down into the car seat before sliding into her again. Her head falls back and her fingers tangle in my hair as she sinks down on me, taking all of me into herself with such blissful generosity.

It's incredible what her body can do, how she can part for me and yet still squeeze me so tightly, her sheath rippling as she moves. I find that I want to throw her onto her back and mate her with all the force in my body.

I shake my head to clear the cobwebs away. *That* is not what this is, either. The instinct to mate and claim is natural for orcs, of course, but I have long since reined in those instincts. I will never form a mate bond with anyone. I don't need that kind of commitment, that sort of all-consuming restriction. My life is about work, about business, and about the freedom to do both.

Gritting my teeth, I restrain the urge and try to focus only on Ms. Kristoff on top of me, her thighs flexing as she lifts herself up and then sinks back down on my cock. It's a wonder that my little assistant is in my lap, her breasts jiggling under her blouse every time I thrust up into her. She's bracing herself against me, her legs clearly tiring as she does the majority of the work.

I take over because my need has grown immense, almost painful. Now I'm cupping her ass with both hands, lifting her up until my cock nearly leaves her, then dropping her down again. She takes all of it, her moans climbing even as she tries to hold them in.

"It's all right," I murmur to her, pushing some sweaty hair back from her face. "George won't tell."

She's not close enough, though, not as close to the brink as I am, and I'm not the kind of orc who has sex with a female and doesn't get her there. So I lift her up with one hand, then reach down between us to play with her clit some more. She writhes and whimpers as I tease her, pushing in shallowly and then pulling back. As she shivers, so does she tighten around me, which is just what I needed.

I slam into her roughly, and Ms. Kristoff lets out the most beautiful cry. Now I'm really fucking her, my own arms shaking with the impending force of my climax. I'm going to shoot so much into her again. It's building and building, and my balls are tightening, and I'm gritting my teeth as Ms. Kristoff's voice climbs.

"You're so filthy," I tell her, still strumming her clit as I bring her up and down on my lap. "Taking my cock for the second time today."

"Yes, I am." She barely gets the words out between panting breaths. "It's so good."

"You like it? Taking my fat dick? Your pussy is going to be so used."

She nods feverishly, her fingers digging into my scalp, and I think she might just be made for me.

I can't help it anymore. I'm so close that I'm growling as I fuck her faster, and I can already feel it moving through me, the sheer pleasure so intense I'm nearly blinded by it. But then, Ms. Kristoff clamps down hard, and she lets out a sharp cry.

There we are. I unleash at the same time that she crests, and I can't help a painful-sounding groan from escaping my lips as I plunge into her, spewing everything. Fuck, it's glorious as she milks me, her pulsing making me spurt again, and then again. I didn't think I had so much cum to give.

Gasping, Ms. Kristoff collapses against me, her arms weaving around my neck as her head rests on my shoulder. It's intimate, but I don't have the heart to separate us yet. I suppose I can let her gather herself for a moment.

"Thank you," I hear her whisper in my ear. She sighs and her weight sinks into me, which isn't much.

I don't know what to say back, so I choose to say nothing, though I feel like I ought to. After a few moments, Ms. Kristoff releases me, sitting back while still speared on my cock. Worst of all, it's somehow still hard for her, even though I just had the most intense orgasm of my life.

Her hazel eyes peer up at me like she's looking for something, but I don't know what. After a moment of silence, her brows furrow, and then she lifts herself up and I slip out of her. She doesn't try to clean up, so my cum gets all over the seat as she looks for her pantyhose and underwear. Then she turns away from me to put them on, so I can't see her face.

Something feels strange as she finishes, then smooths her skirt back down into place. Ms. Kristoff returns to her own seat and snaps in her seatbelt like nothing happened. Her pantyhose are a disaster, but we are dropping her off at home, so she doesn't have far to go.

She takes out her phone and pulls up my calendar for tomorrow, her eyes laser-focused on it. Usually she has flawless posture, but her shoulders seem tight, her neck bent as we approach her apartment.

"Goodnight, Mr. Roth," she says as she gets out of the car, like she always does. Her expression is blank. "See you tomorrow."

After she's gone, I realize I forgot to tell her about the gala next weekend. I'll need her to come with me, as she always does.

"George, stop the car."

He does as he's told, putting on the brake before leaving the curb. I throw open the door and step out, finding Ms. Kristoff putting in her keycode to get into her apartment building.

"Ms. Kristoff, wait."

She spins around, her eyes wide, her mouth slightly open.

"Mr. Roth?" She sounds almost hopeful. "What... what is it?"

"Next Saturday, I need you to come with me to the Humane Society gala."

Her face falls.

"Oh, all right." Ms. Kristoff sighs and nods. "Anything else?"

She seems almost... impatient with me, which I haven't experienced before. But I suppose this is her off-time, and I've just interrupted her trying to go home with cum-soaked pantyhose.

"That's all."

I watch as she lets herself into the building, then slams the door closed behind her.

Hmm.

Back in the car, George knows better than to say anything about what he heard earlier. He's my own personal driver, not employed by the company, so he's loyal only to me. I don't want to think about what would happen if it got out that I was fucking my personal assistant.

That thought is sobering. Delicious though she is, what we have is temporary. Once I've gotten what I need, once I've had my fill of her, I'll cut it off. She's more valuable to me as an employee than as a sexual partner, and I've been foolish for taking it this far.

My cock sure doesn't like the sound of that,

though. In fact, my entire being riots at the idea of losing what we've gained. She was marvelous today, pliant and yet thirsty, eager and happy to be humiliated. She liked everything I did to her, everything I said to her. She leaned against me at the end, tender in a way I didn't expect.

Maybe this has all been a mistake, because it will be hard to end it.

CHAPTER
NINE

ROSETTE

As the haze of sex drifted off and I lay against Mr. Roth on the back seat, I'd hoped he would put his arms around me. That he would say something to me, something kind, perhaps. Something that meant he didn't really believe I was a filthy slut, or whatever he had called me.

But he didn't, and that was what made me feel truly dirty.

I throw my pantyhose in the trash along with my underwear, then climb into the shower. I scrub every last inch of myself, then use plenty of products on my skin and hair before getting out.

This is what I wanted, and yet I'm furious at myself now for wanting it. Today was incredible, exactly what I hoped for. Everything I could have dreamed of—getting fucked against Mr. Roth's desk, riding his lap in the car.

Right now, though, I feel like I was emotionally run over by a truck.

After throwing together a quick stir-fry, I flop down on the couch. Usually I try to get to the gym, maybe see some of my friends, but tonight I just want to vegetate and mope.

I fall asleep watching some crime show, which is much more soothing than you'd think.

Then I'm up again the next day, trying to put on my game face. Be a good assistant and definitely don't catch feelings for your boss.

The car is, surprisingly, a couple of minutes late to pick me up. When I get in the back, Mr. Roth sits in his usual seat, his arms crossed, that focused frown on his face. As always, I pull out my phone and look at the calendar, reading off a list of our first few appointments.

When I'm finished, though, Mr. Roth actually speaks to me.

"I have something for you, Ms. Kristoff."

I watch with curiosity as he reaches into the footwell and picks up a paper bag, which he then passes to me. I open it up to peer inside to find a new pair of black tights and a skimpy red lingerie set, much like what I was wearing yesterday.

Replacements for the underwear he ruined.

I'm not sure what to think of it. Mr. Roth has never given me a gift before.

"Oh, thank you," I say. Maybe I misread him yesterday. Maybe he simply doesn't know how to show his emotions.

Mr. Roth grunts and turns his head away to look out the window.

When we've finished the morning appointments, we return to the office for a few hours to attend some corporate meetings. These are Mr. Roth's least favorite, and he always comes out of them in a bad mood.

"Waste of time," he'll say with a distasteful curl of his lip. But it's a requirement, and one he can't skip.

I wait in his office, typing up notes to occupy myself. When Mr. Roth storms back into the room, he looks even more annoyed than usual.

"Quarterly reports," he snarls, slamming his office door behind him so hard that I worry it'll shatter the glass. I think it's actually plastic, though.

"I'll set aside time." I scroll through the calendar, looking for a few hours I can mark off for working on them. While I'm busy with my task, Mr. Roth lowers the curtains to his office, blocking us from sight.

This time, he grabs me by the ass and sits me on the very edge of the desk, lifting my thighs up as he settles his massive waist between them. I'm still accustomed to him from yesterday, so he fits in easily, sighing with contentment as he buries himself in me up to the hilt.

I keep my voice down as he fucks me against the desk, the whole thing creaking with the force of his thrusts. He makes sure that I get there, too, pausing to rub my clit as he takes me, but I don't come like a freight train the way I did yesterday.

Again, he gives me a single tissue to clean up and insists I don't wipe off the rest. He sniffs the air as he opens the curtains again, then returns to his desk chair, continuing with his day as if nothing happened.

I settle back in my seat, pretending everything is normal when the receptionist comes in to ask a question. This should all be my ideal situation—getting fucked like I've always wanted by my boss during the day, working my job at night. So why does Mr. Roth treating this so casually... kind of hurt?

The week continues that way, on into the next. I don't see him at all that weekend at Octavio's, which makes me certain of what I already knew: that all I'm good for is a warm body. He has no need of Velvet anymore.

On Thursday afternoon, I say goodbye like I always do when George drops me off at my apartment, then head up to get changed and ready for Octavio's. I barely have the heart for it, though. If a client wants to go to a back room tonight, I might not have it in me.

I'm not surprised at all when Mr. Roth doesn't show up. I spend my time with other clients, trying to stay focused on conversations, trying to enjoy it when they touch me the way I like to be touched. It's always been a pleasure of mine to be used, to be passed around and groped and fondled. To be watched and seen and enjoyed.

But I find I miss him. I miss the orc who showed up just to eat me out, just to bury his face in my pussy. I'll probably never see him at Octavio's again, now that I'm his toy at work.

Oh well. I should have known from the beginning that's what this was. I need to get with the program. There's nothing for me with my boss, and besides—I don't need anything else. I have everything I could want between my two jobs. Maybe I have to keep what we do a secret during the day, but I get to be seen all night.

It's probably better this way. Less complicated.

I'm sitting on one man's lap while his friend feels up my tits. They're enjoying watching each other play with me when someone massive steps into the VIP room. Someone who commands the attention of everyone there.

It's Mr. Roth, and within moments, he's looming over us like the shadow of a mountain, his lips curled down into a devastating scowl.

"Vincent," I say, sitting upright. For a moment, I feel ashamed that he's seeing me like this, engaged with two other men. But then I remember this is my job, and he knows that. I have no reason to be ashamed when he came here as a client himself once upon a time.

"Who are you?" the first man says to our visitor. I think he said his name was John or something like that. He grips my hips where I sit on his lap. "We're a little busy here."

Vincent's brows lower dangerously over his eyes, and he makes a noise I can only describe as a snarl. "Get your hands off her."

The second man in the party quickly releases my tits, intimidated by the huge orc standing over us. But John isn't going to back down so easily.

"I'm paying good money for this," he snaps, which is bold for a human in the face of an orc who could snap him in half without trying. "Go find your own girl."

Vincent leans closer, his sharp, dangerous tusks jutting out of his massive jaw. "She's *mine*." He reaches toward the man as if to grab him by the throat, but reflexively, I knock his hand away.

How dare he come in here while I'm working and scare off my clients? He already gets me five days a week. And he's never once claimed I was *his* at the office.

He's made it very clear to me what we are.

"Stop it." I glare daggers to get my message across. "I'm not yours."

Vincent retracts his hand, curling it into a fist, and opens his mouth to argue—but I narrow my eyes, waiting for him to contradict me.

"This is my job, Vincent," I say, staying firmly in my seat on John's lap. "You know that."

"But Velvet—"

"But nothing. Leave us alone."

Vincent's eyes widen as he stands up straighter, both of his hands flexing at his sides. I think he wants to lay into my two clients with said fists, so I say, "You aren't entitled to me. If you don't like it, then leave."

Already though, the second man who'd been groping me is paying his bill in cash and getting up. John scoots me off his lap and follows suit, neither of them wanting to get into a tussle with a seven-foot orc.

"Wait!" I call out to them.

"Sorry, we're not here for competition." John slaps his money on the table and doesn't glance back at me when he leaves.

Now I'm alone, and my anger's building. This could have been a really profitable night for me with two people to entertain, and now I have no one.

I glare at Vincent. "What are you doing?" I demand, rising to my feet. "You scared them off!"

"So? They weren't worthy of you anyway." His face doesn't show a shred of regret.

"That's not the point! They were paying customers."

He frowns deeper. "I can pay you more."

I grind my teeth together at how dense he's acting. This isn't just a job for me. It's *fun* for me, to be lusted after by so many people. And now he's ruining it.

"What are you even doing here?" I ask miserably, falling back into a seat at the table. "I thought you weren't going to come back."

He furrows his brow, and he sits down in the chair beside me. "Why wouldn't I come to see Velvet?"

"Because now you get everything you want from Rosette."

That crease gets deeper. "Everything I want," he echoes.

I sigh, putting my face in my hands. "If those guys complain to my boss, I could lose this job."

"Then I'll give you a raise," Vincent says, putting a hand on my back.

I shake him off. "You don't get it. I don't do it for the money."

It's like I've spoken a foreign language to him, the way he searches my face for answers. "Then why do you do it?"

"Because I *enjoy* it!" I want to stomp my foot. "Because I like being wanted by people. Being seen."

"But I see you all day," he says, leaning closer. "And you're wanted. All day. By me."

Now he's sparking a fury in me. How can he act like this is something more than it is, when he's made it clear where I stand?

"All this 'mine' bullshit?" I say, pushing him away. "Nobody owns me. Especially not you."

Vincent recoils as if I've slapped him.

"You can't deny it," he says. "You rode my cock just a few hours ago."

I can't stand it anymore. Suddenly, I don't care if he's my boss. He's intruded on my space and scared off my customers, on top of treating me like his own personal prostitute. Now he wants to control me outside of work, too?

"Get out," I say in a low voice. "I want you to leave."

He stares at me. "You don't mean that."

"I do." I wave a hand at the bouncer, who

rises from his seat. "Go. Before security shows you out."

Vincent might be a big guy, but the bouncers at Octavio's don't play around. They'll swarm him like flies until he goes down if he causes any trouble.

My boss stares at me like he doesn't recognize me, then rises to his feet. He holds up his hands as the bouncer approaches.

"I'm leaving," he grumbles, shoving past the big centaur. Vincent shoots me one last infuriated look before storming out of the VIP room.

Now I've lost my business for the night, and who knows what he'll do to me at work tomorrow? I wonder if I've just destroyed my own career for this stupid gig.

"You all right?" the bouncer asks. "I thought you and that orc were chummy."

"Not anymore. And he should go on the list." It's a ledger of people no longer allowed into Octavio's.

Though he's surprised, the bouncer doesn't argue with me. Now I won't have to worry about seeing Mr. Roth here again. And at least if I get fired from my day job, I'll still have this and my savings to keep me afloat.

Fuck. This night went as poorly as possible. I hope I haven't made a huge mistake.

CHAPTER
TEN

VINCENT

'm so shocked at first by Velvet kicking me out that it takes some minutes for my rage to fully boil to the surface. It doesn't happen until after I've stepped out of Octavio's and onto the street that my entire body begins shaking with my wrath.

How could she say that? After how I've claimed her this many times, covered her in my smell, shown her pleasure so great she screamed? She is mine. Only mine. And her denial is like a sharp blade in my gut. How could she ignore what we have and act as if it means nothing to her?

Though my orcish fire is burning bright, I close my eyes as I wait for George to arrive and breathe the cold air in through my nose. I need to calm myself before I act irrationally.

Perhaps what enrages me most is that she was right to do it, to demand that I leave. This is her place of work. I know what she does here. But I couldn't help losing my temper at the sight of another person's hands all over her. I'm an orc, and orcs protect what belongs to us.

My plan to keep a distance between us clearly has not worked. I've grown far too attached to my pretty assistant, that much is obvious. Now my instincts are all ablaze, demanding to know why she's back there in that club surrounded by roaming hands.

I'm still seething as the car arrives, but I've gotten it under my control enough that it doesn't show on my face. As always, George silently drives me home.

I remember every word she said. *Now you get everything you want from Rosette.*

It makes me angrier that this is how she sees it. I had stayed away from Octavio's because I didn't want to jeopardize her, to take up all of her time, but I couldn't any longer. I wanted to see Velvet again.

I should never have gone.

Though it's already late, there's no sleeping for me. I head down to the basement gym, where I beat my sandbag until the seams are snapping. All I have to do is think about Velvet on that stranger's lap, dismembered hands fondling her perfect tits—which I haven't even seen for myself before tonight—and my pulse skyrockets. My punch rips through the leather casing, sending sand flying everywhere.

Damn it.

I return to my room, reminding myself to ask Ms. Kristoff about getting that cleaned up. She can make the arrangements.

It's not until then that I think, *What if she doesn't come in to work tomorrow? What if she isn't standing on the curb when I arrive to pick her up?*

What if she quits?

It's only thanks to three more strong whiskeys and a game of Gekaran that I'm able to fall asleep.

I'm wearing my sunglasses today to mask the bags under my eyes as we pull up in front of Ms. Kristoff's apartment the next morning. She is dutifully standing where she always stands, but today...

Today, she is wearing pants.

I've never ever seen her in pants. Since her very first interview she's worn pencil skirts, showing off her shapely legs. Today, though, black slacks cover her ass and hang down all the way to her heels.

I watch as she slides into the car, putting her purse in the seat back pocket and buckling in. She takes out her phone to look at the calendar, the same as she does every morning.

But she's in pants.

"Ten a.m., meeting with the Sandhill investors," she begins, reading off the next few items on the calendar.

"I need a cleaning crew at my house," I interrupt. She pauses but doesn't look at me as she pulls up her notes app and jots down my request. Then she continues with the schedule for the day.

Besides the pants, Ms. Kristoff behaves perfectly normal the entire morning. She is attentive, focused, and doesn't leave room for error. She makes calls as we drive, scheduling the cleaners, and then arranging to have a new punching bag delivered. At lunch, we have a brief reprieve from meetings when we settle down at one of my favorite restaurants.

"I'll have the pork chop," I say to the waiter, "and she'll have the—"

"Club sandwich, please," Ms. Kristoff interrupts. She hands the waiter her menu, not once looking at me.

My mouth snaps shut. I return my menu, too, and the waiter leaves us.

Ms. Kristoff says nothing, and so neither do I. It's not as if we ever made idle conversation before, but now the silence feels cavernous. I don't know what I would expect her to say, but she stares straight ahead, drinking her water, occasionally glancing at her phone as she receives text messages.

"Four o'clock rescheduled," she says.

"All right."

She devours her club sandwich, and I watch her through my sunglasses. She will not tolerate what I did last night. She is firmly putting her foot down, and I am both intrigued and annoyed. I don't think I'll be taking her against the desk today.

The rest of the afternoon is much the same. Ms. Kristoff is impeccably professional, and there's not a fault to find. Any idle time she spends dutifully ignoring me and working.

When we stop for an afternoon coffee, George glances at me in the rearview mirror, one eyebrow arched.

"Pardon me for overstepping," he says, "but Ms. Kristoff appears... upset. Should I arrange for some flowers, perhaps?"

I snarl through my tusks. "You are overstepping."

But George doesn't appear shaken. He has been my driver for a long time.

I think for a moment about those goddamned *pants*, and how she ordered her own lunch. How not even a bit of her personality shone through today, as if she had erected a bulletproof wall between us.

"Flowers may not be a bad idea," I allow. I need her back, my Ms. Kristoff from before. The one who took my cock so eagerly and then rested her weight on me after I'd made her scream. I should have held her then, shown her what she's come to mean to me. Then she would never doubt that she's mine.

That's when the truth settles on me, the full knowing of it. I truly have claimed her. My instincts are clamoring for her, to have her by my side, and I need her with me again.

"She will be attending the gala with you tomorrow night, correct?" George asks.

Normally, Ms. Kristoff comes as my assistant, keeping to the sidelines. She does not partake or enjoy, there only to take notes and make follow-up appointments.

"You could give them to her then," he suggests.

Damn it, it's a good idea. I grind my teeth because this will require one thing, one thing that I have so far in my life refused to give out to anyone.

An apology. And that may not be enough to get into her good graces again. No, if I am to have Ms. Kristoff back, I will need to put myself out on the table. Show her that things have changed for me, that simply being Mr. Roth isn't enough.

When we bring Ms. Kristoff back to her apartment that night, I stop her from getting out with a gentle hand on her arm. Her eyes dart up to mine, suspicious.

"Tomorrow night. I am... sending you a gift. Do not bring your notebook."

Her lips twist. "But how else will I take notes?"

"You will not be taking notes." With that, I release her, and she departs the car with a perplexed look on her face.

ROSETTE

I am protecting my peace.

That's what I told myself all day today as I did my job dutifully and efficiently. I am protecting my peace. I am going to work so hard and do so well that Mr. Roth will have no reason to fire me, but I will not give him another inch into my life, either.

But then, he told me not to bring my notebook tomorrow night. What does that mean? What kind of gift is he sending me?

Much to my relief, he does not come to Octavio's that night. But the next morning, Saturday, I awaken to the doorbell ringing.

On the other side of my front door is a woman wearing a Hartmann's tag from the department store downtown. She's carrying a bag in her arms attached to a hanger, and she passes it to me when I sleepily open the door.

"From Mr. Roth, for the event tonight," she says, then departs without another word.

What on earth could this be?

I carry the package inside and drape it over my chair, then zip open the bag. Inside is a beautiful blue dress with a metallic shine to the fabric, making it look like a cut sapphire, with a matching set of earrings clipped to the tag.

Is this Mr. Roth's gift?

I pull it out, and it's got four tiny straps that look like they'll crisscross over my chest and back. It will show off quite a bit of my cleavage with its swooping collar.

I've never worn something like this in my life. I've dressed as Velvet, sure, but not as a high-class woman with real sapphire jewelry.

This is not what an assistant wears. This is what a *date* would wear.

I stare at the dress for a long time, wondering if he's saying what I think he's saying. That he wants to be more.

After getting in my workout for the day and taking a long shower, I stare at the dress a while longer, then finally decide to change into it. I do my makeup to match, using a deep blue eye shadow and thick eyeliner to really accentuate it, then brush mascara into my lashes. Finally, I apply a brown-burgundy lip stain instead of red to let my eyes stand out.

At six p.m. on the dot, I'm waiting at the curb when Mr. Roth's car arrives. I slide into the back, this time keeping my small black clutch in my lap.

The car doesn't pull away immediately. No, when I close the door behind me, I turn to see Mr. Roth sitting in his seat, a rather large bouquet of flowers in his hands. He's dressed in a perfectly white suit, clearly custom made for his frame, with a black collared shirt and red tie. He looks sharper than a knife.

"Ms. Kristoff." The way he says my name is intentional and defined. "I wanted to express my regrets for my actions the other night."

My mouth is probably hanging open. This is a set of words I never expected.

He hands the flowers to me, and dumbfounded into silence, I take them. They're roses, white and red ones with a few black scattered among the mix. They are sexy and they smell delicious, and I can't believe that *Mr. Vincent Roth himself* just gave them to me.

To apologize.

"Oh." I don't know what else to say. "All... right."

Mr. Roth quirks an eyebrow but doesn't press me for more. I sit back in the seat, holding the roses against my chest.

We arrive at the venue a few minutes later, and George drops us off out front. Typically, I go around the back of these types of events while Mr. Roth exits the car and enters publicly, but this time, he reaches out and takes my hand in his.

"Bring the flowers," he says. "They'll look good in the photos."

Photos? He wants me to be in the photos with him?

He pulls me out of the car, and I allow myself to be pulled.

All at once, cameras are snapping. This is a big, hoity-toity fundraiser for the biggest humane society in the country, and the paparazzi want to know who's coming. And I'm on Vincent Roth's arm.

My throat tightens as Vincent curls my hand around his elbow, then squeezes it. I really am here as his date. He's claiming me publicly, for everyone to see.

We enter through the front doors, where a camera is waiting for us to pose in front of a big wall. Easily, Mr. Roth slides his arm around my back and holds me against him as the camera goes off, capturing us for all eternity.

He doesn't release me as we step away from the camera and slide into the venue. A sign for the cocktail hour points straight ahead, and Mr. Roth leads me with him. He surveys the room, the way he always does at these events, trying to discern who best to mingle with to achieve his personal ends. Networking with other bigwigs is always at the top of his list.

I follow along behind, depositing the flowers on a table as we go while he heads for his first target, an older guy I recognize from other fancy-pants events we've attended. After Mr. Roth reintroduces himself—I remember this man's name now, Mr. Schwarz—I take out my phone so I can jot down notes. Instead, though, Mr. Roth tugs me by the arm and brings me in against his side.

"And this is Ms. Kristoff," he says. "Accompanying me this evening."

The man's eyebrows jump. "Oh, you've brought a date for once, have you, Mr. Roth? I didn't think anyone could pique your interest. I've always seen you as a bit of a loner."

"I suppose it just takes the right person." Mr. Roth squeezes my side before releasing me. "Then you know you're caught."

CHAPTER
ELEVEN

ROSETTE

'm not sure what Mr. Roth is thinking. Many of his colleagues from the firm are at this event, too. Surely they'll catch wind if he's walking around introducing me to people as his date.

I feel like I'm on a train that's about to crash.

"What are you doing?" I hiss at him as we finally leave our conversation with Mr. Schwarz and head toward the bar. "Human resources is going to have some things to say."

"I'll deal with it," he says with finality. "What would you like to drink?"

I'm surprised that he's even asking me, when

at any other gala, he's ordered me a gin and soda with lime.

"Wine," I say, because I do actually like gin and soda, but I want to assert myself. "White wine, please."

Mr. Roth nods and gives the bartender our order: one white wine and one dry martini with two olives. Both are produced in short order, and then we return to mingling.

I don't fight it when Mr. Roth slides his arm around my waist because truthfully... I like it. If I thought I didn't mean anything to him before the night he burst into Octavio's, that thought is banished. He's here telling me—and everyone else around us—that I'm his. He's saying it loudly and clearly.

I'm still not sure how I feel about that, whether I *want* to be his. But the idea is appealing, standing here on Mr. Roth's arm as we chat to his society acquaintances, and they politely ask me questions like, "Where did you go to school?" I answer with my backwater state university, but no one bats an eyelash.

"How did you two meet?"

Here it comes.

"She began working as my assistant," Mr.

Roth says smoothly. "But it became something more than that."

Where I expect the couple we're talking with to be disgusted, instead, they both nod in understanding.

"We also met at work," the wife says. "Though more as colleagues."

The husband arches an eyebrow. "Got up to some extracurricular activities on the job?"

I can feel it when my entire face turns red, because I feel like my head is about to pop off my body from the embarrassment. But Mr. Roth just chuckles, neither agreeing nor disagreeing. He takes my hand in his and squeezes it, and then he doesn't let go.

Eventually, we move on, making our way around the room. When the cocktail hour is over, we're herded to our seats in the massive ballroom, where I find we've been seated with others from the firm—including the CEO. Mr. Roth pulls out my chair for me, then takes my hand as I sit. He kisses the back of it before letting go, and my face must turn bright red all over. Not even the light show on the walls or the beautiful, glittering centerpieces can distract me from the fact we're blatantly ignoring human resources protocol.

"And who is this?" the CEO asks. Naomi Philips is a force to be reckoned with, and I'm squeezing Mr. Roth's hand so tight under the table that I'm probably biting into his skin with my nails.

He looks unfazed.

"Ms. Kristoff, my assistant. I believe you've met before."

Her brow rises. "Your assistant? From the firm?" She surveys me. "Well, I hope you're taking good notes."

I open my mouth, not sure what to say in response when I have my phone nowhere near me, but she simply chuckles.

"And what's your excuse, Vincent?" Naomi says. "For dating your assistant."

He shrugs. "The mating exemption."

The table falls totally quiet. Every conversation comes to a halt as our coworkers turn their heads to stare.

Oh, no.

"Really?" Naomi gapes at him. "You?"

Without hesitation, Mr. Roth nods. "We'll be approaching human resources on Monday."

We will? This is news to me. As is, apparently, that he'll be claiming the mating exemption.

Which only means one thing. He thinks *I'm* his mate.

My jaw works as the music slows, then stops, and someone comes on stage to start speaking. Naomi turns away, as does everyone else at the table, to watch the speaker extoll the virtues of the organization.

"Are you serious?" I lean my head in close to Mr. Roth's side as I whisper. "When were you going to tell me?"

"Tonight." His hand curls tighter around mine. "I'm sorry for the way it came out."

But I don't think he's sorry. I think he engineered it so he could catch me off guard in public, so I wouldn't be able to freak out on him the way I am freaking out inside my head.

How long has he known? What does orcish mating even entail?

I move to get up from my chair, and Mr. Roth gives me a quizzical look.

"I need to go to the bathroom," I say, and immediately, he gets to his feet with me and guides me out of the ballroom. We ask a volunteer to point us in the right direction.

But I pass the bathrooms and duck down into a side hallway. Mr. Roth glances around us, where only a harried-looking volunteer is carrying an auction basket, and she runs on ahead, leaving us alone.

"You can't make stuff up like that," I say immediately. "That's just to throw them off the scent, right?"

"No."

Mr. Roth's gaze is solid, unwavering.

"Really?" I choke. "With me? But..."

"You're my mate." His tone couldn't be more certain. "Mine."

VINCENT

Now she knows, with no room for doubt.

My first clue should have been when I threatened a man just for touching Velvet's tits. And then, last night, I imagined her at Octavio's. Imagined what she might be doing there. The longer I pictured it, strangers' hands all over her, maybe even some other cock inside her, I was sure I was going to break a hole in my brick walls.

Instead, I destroyed another punching bag.

It was when I tore through the leather and stitching again, and it collapsed to the floor in a heap, that I knew. My body and soul had both laid claim to Rosette Kristoff. What I thought was a tryst with my assistant has become much, much more than that.

For me, at least.

This is, most unfavorably, an orcish experience. Only orcs, wolfmen, and a few other scattered species out there spontaneously imprint on their mates, creating an undeniable and everlasting bond. Often it springs from attraction, but sometimes it can come even for totally platonic work colleagues.

Thus, the mating exemption. I can't control who my body imprints on. Though I'm sure we helped it along by fucking the way we did.

The one question mark has been how Ms. Kristoff will respond. I am asking her, quite plainly, to be with me. To be mine forever, wholly and completely.

Which, after how I've behaved, is a big request.

"Don't I get a say in this?" she asks, pulling her hand away from mine.

I furrow my brow, confused by her question.

"The mate bond only happens once in a lifetime, with one person," I say patiently. "It's destiny."

She keeps her clutch close to her, like I might try to take it. "You didn't answer my question. I'm a human, not an orc. You decided I'm your mate, whatever that means—"

"Whatever that means? It is a serious thing, mating. I don't have a choice in it."

She screws up her lips. "But I have a choice, don't I?"

It hits me like a punch to the gut, what she's saying. She's suggesting that she won't accept it. That she wants to deny the truth about us.

I straighten, adjusting my red tie. Losing my temper now won't do me any favors. She needs something else, something more... tender, I believe. I need to convince her that she wants to be my mate.

"Ms. Kristoff." I take a step toward her, then go down onto one knee. Her eyes get big as I gently scoop up her hand in mine. "No. *Rosette*."

I see the shiver as it rolls up her body.

"Please, give me tonight. Let me show you, tonight, what being my mate could be like." I bring her fingers to my lips, and I think how even now, I've never kissed her. If she lets me, I will rectify that this very evening.

Her mouth falls open, revealing the tip of her pink tongue. She wets her lips with it, staring down at me with wide eyes. I think I have pushed her just a tad off-balance.

"Really, Vincent?"

I preen at the way she uses my first name.

"You're going to get on your knees?" She shakes her head. "You never struck me as dramatic."

"There are moments that call for it."

Her uncertainty as she chews her lip is delicious, so close to agreeing. If she lets me, I know that I can give her a good life. A very good life.

"All right," she says at last. "Show me, then."

I surge to my feet and whirl her into my arms as the last word leaves her lips, and she lets out a surprised squeak as I encircle her. She vanishes inside my embrace, right where she belongs, and I wish I could keep her there for all time. I lean down to kiss her temple.

"You know what mates do, don't you?" I ask her, her hair tangling around my tusk as I lower my head even more. "After all the dancing is over."

"I... I think I do."

"Good." I release her, rising back to my full height. "Then let's go back to the party."

"I still need to pee," she pouts, so I hold her bag and wait as she goes.

Ms. Kristoff is reserved when she returns, but when I hold out my elbow, she loops her hand through it, and we head back to the ballroom together. She's elegance incarnate in the blue dress I chose for her.

We slip into our seats while an inspirational video of rescued pets plays on the screen. I skim her thigh with my palm, and she shivers under it. I know that despite how she turned me away at Octavio's, she is undeniably attracted to me. She's wanted me since we met, same as I have her.

Why it took us so long to get here is a mystery to me, but I'll convince her the destination is worthwhile.

Then dinner is served, and I watch from the corner of my eye to ensure she's getting enough. I plan to keep her up into the late, late hours tonight. My coworkers make conversation, which she easily picks up. I can see the parts of her that are Velvet as she asks questions and uses a higher-pitched voice. This is the version of her that she uses to entertain and socialize.

I am still very curious to learn who the true Ms. Kristoff is.

Then, at last, the dinner is cleared away and bidding games are played for dessert. As a cream pie goes past, Ms. Kristoff sits up abruptly.

"Is that chocolate cream?" she asks, fascinated by it.

"I think so."

She urges me to bid, so I hold up my paddle when the pie goes up for auction. Another woman and her husband at a different table are also eager for it, so I end up forking over a few thousand dollars for a pie we probably could buy from a grocery store for significantly less.

But Rosette is immensely pleased and eats a surprising amount—two whole pieces—before giving up and collapsing back in her chair. She smiles up at me, and I think my heart stops in my chest.

"Thank you."

"For the cats and dogs," I say.

"Would you ever want a dog?"

I quirk my head down at her. She's got her hand on top of mine where it rests on her thigh, and I rub the fabric of her dress there.

"I like dogs well enough. Growing up, we used them for hunting."

She arches an eyebrow. "Hunting?"

"Orcs love to hunt. But a pet dog? I have never had one."

Ms. Kristoff smiles wistfully. "I'd love to have a dog. But I'm never home. I wouldn't want it to be waiting for me alone while I'm at work all day and then some nights."

But I could give that to her.

It arises unbidden. I remember the time she mentioned how she wished someone else would do her laundry, and I could make that happen, too, if she lived in my home with me.

I try not to let my little fantasy run away with me. I need to show her what I can offer her in a way that won't overwhelm her. She clearly values her independence and agency, so I'll have to tread carefully.

As I file this information away for later, the live auction begins. Ms. Kristoff seems most bored by this, disinterested in the fancy trips to Thailand where you can ride elephants, or the all-expenses-paid beach getaways.

"Sometimes a girl just wants a dinner at Red Robin," she mutters as the bidding goes on. But breathing in her scent, I am nearly ready for this to be over.

At last, the auction ends, and the lights dim. I sweep her up into my arms the moment the music starts, and she giggles in a way that's surprisingly carefree as other couples come out to join us.

"I didn't know you liked to dance," she says, falling easily into step with me. "You're pretty okay at it."

"I took classes."

"To learn to dance?"

"I had a phase. I learned two kinds of dancing, pottery, and baseball."

"Baseball," she repeats, squinting. "I have a hard time imagining that."

"I wasn't good at it."

I bring her in closer until her cheek rests against my chest. She sighs and leans in, letting her arms wrap around my waist. We sway to the music together, and the tightness in my ribs eases having her so near me.

This is good. This is the balm my soul needed.

Is this what it's like, to have a mate? To hold them close and feel as if all is right in the world?

I could get used to it.

CHAPTER
TWELVE

ROSETTE

Vincent Roth holds me like I'm something deeply precious to him. His hand curls around mine, his arm at my waist, his heart beating huge and heavy against my cheek.

"Rosette." The way he says my name is silken. I don't think I've ever heard him speak it aloud before. "I want to know you."

Tilting my head, I peer up at him. "Know me? You know me already. Both versions of me."

"Yes, but I sense there are three."

He might not be wrong about that. I do play a certain version of myself at work, and a different one at Octavio's. But who is Rosette without either at play?

"I don't know if I've ever been that version of myself since moving to this city," I say after a time. "The one who's just Rosette."

He lifts his hand to my hair, threading his fingers through it. "I guess we will have to find her and lure her out." Leaning down, he noses my hair and inhales. All at once, I can feel his cock against me through his nice suit pants, but he continues dancing as if nothing has changed.

"Who is Vincent?" I ask after a while. "I know he enjoys learning new things."

He shrugs. "I don't know that there is one."

"Surely there is. A Vincent who isn't Mr. Roth."

He rubs one of his tusks thoughtfully. "I've always wanted to go up. Up, and up, and up." He shakes his head. "Then I saw you. You walked into my office for your interview, and then it all became about you."

What?

I stare up into his face, not quite believing what I heard. "When you interviewed me?"

"You're all I've thought about since." He leans down, cupping my chin in his hand so I can't turn away, and looks right into my eyes.

"I've been obsessed with you, Rosette. Perhaps that's who Vincent really is. The orc who cannot get his mate out of his head."

It's as if an electric current has been sent through me.

"Would you... like to go back to my house with me?" Vincent asks.

Oh, right. *What mates do*, he said. I think I might have an idea of what that means after the night he's shown me, and now I want to find out.

"All right. Let's go. I need to get these heels off my feet."

He shoots off a message to George on his phone before tucking it away in his pocket, then he leads me out of the ballroom. We wave goodbye to his coworkers as we go, who all turn to murmur to each other the moment we step out.

We'll be the talk of the office for a while.

Then we head into the cool night air, which I'm immensely grateful for after all the wine I've had. Vincent simply holds my hand as we stand on the curb, waiting for George to arrive. When the black SUV slides into the pickup area, Vincent opens the car door for me and helps me inside before going around to the other door.

"The house, please," Vincent says to George.

The driver glances at me in the rearview mirror, nods, and drives off.

We don't talk as we leave the city, but our hands stay linked, Vincent's thumb gently brushing over my knuckles. As the road narrows along the river, George turns off into a driveway at an enormous, beautiful house.

Wow. Big bay windows look out at the street and then the river, and we first enter through a gate into a quaint yard, clearly maintained by a professional gardener. A wide-set door welcomes us inside.

The ceilings are vaulted, the interior decoration mostly white and minimalist. There are accents of black and red throughout, with black countertops and white cupboards, and paintings with red splatters and black-and-white photographs.

It is very much a Vincent Roth home, if I were to have imagined one.

The living room is sprawling, with a television hanging from the ceiling. Another big window looks out over the river and the city beyond it, immense buildings on the skyline.

"Do you want a drink?" Vincent asks, leading me into the kitchen.

"I think I've had enough tonight." I scratch

my cheek. "I'm actually a bit of a lightweight. I don't drink at Octavio's, and when I do go out, I only need one or two to feel tipsy."

Vincent's lip quirks. "All right. Then I suppose there's nothing to do but to take you to my room." He curls an arm around my back and draws me in closer, tipping his head down so our noses are only a few inches apart. "But there's something I've been wanting to do first."

I cock my head. "What's that?"

He doesn't answer with words. He answers by pressing his much larger lips to mine, his tusks perfectly framing my cheeks. Telling me with a kiss everything he's been holding back.

Vincent's mouth is gentle at first, probing as he caresses me. Damn, he's good at this. His big hand cups the side of my face, tilting me so he can better kiss me.

I melt. I completely, utterly melt, captured by the hopeful sincerity in his lips, in the eagerness and tentative exploration that remind me of being in middle school again. I reach up to wrap my arms around his neck, to bring us even closer together, to squash that distance that's been building up between us.

Now clutching me tight, Vincent tests the seam of my lips, asking for more. I never thought he'd be the type to ask—just take. When my mouth opens, he teases his way in, and immediately I think of all the times I've let other parts of his body inside me this way.

As if in answer, Vincent rubs his hips against me, his cock making itself known at my belly. I return the gesture, telling him just how much I want him, too.

His tongue invades, and this sweet kiss has become a claiming. Hands are all over fabric. I'm tired of wearing this dress, just as I'm tired of his suit getting in the way of feeling his bare skin.

I've never seen Vincent without his clothes on, because he's never done more than lowered his pants. Now, I want to see. I want to *know*.

"Vincent," I say as I pull away from his kiss. He stares down at me with huge, dark pupils. "Where's your room?"

This time, he does smile. It's nothing extravagant, but it's all his, showing his top and bottom teeth and lifting his big tusks to his cheeks.

"This way." He reaches down, slides his hands under me, and lifts me up easily into his arms. I squeak and throw my hands around his neck, worried that he's going to drop me, but Vincent just chuckles.

"I won't let you go."

"I didn't say you would."

"You didn't need to."

He leaves the kitchen, easily carrying my weight, and heads up a set of stairs. They're out in the open, overlooking the living room as we ascend to the second floor. Up here, there's another recreational room, and Vincent pivots down one of the two hallways.

His bedroom is just as minimalist as the rest of the house, with a white and red comforter and black silk sheets. Much like downstairs, the upstairs window looks out over the river. Here, Vincent sets me on the floor on my feet, turning me toward it.

"Look while I undress you," he says. I nod, not moving as he investigates the zipper behind my dress, then pulls it down. Once it's free, he loosens the many straps, sliding them off my shoulders and shuffling the dress down my hips until it's in a pool on the floor. I'm wearing a black lace bra and panty set underneath. Vincent's hands whisper along my sides.

"You're beautiful," he says into my ear. "I could just eat you."

I hope he does.

As I look out over the river, his fingers trail

up my back to the clip of my bra. He unhooks it deftly, and it drops down my arms. His big hands curl around me from behind, scooping up my breasts to hold them both in his massive palms.

"I've been waiting." He gently strokes my nipples with his thumbs, his clothed front hot against my bare skin. "These are magnificent. Perfect for my hands."

I have to agree as he pinches one nipple, rolling it back and forth, little shocks erupting from the spot he's touching me. I twitch and gasp, and Vincent nuzzles the top of my head.

Then one of his hands breaks away, sliding down my belly to the crux of my legs. He slips it down into my underwear, squeezes between my thighs like a heat-seeking missile, and brushes his finger over my soft lower lips.

"Already wet." He chuckles against my hair. "You like being fucked, don't you?"

"I really like it." I swallow. "Especially when it's by you."

He sucks in a sharp breath, pressing his finger between my folds and dragging it up to my clit. He applies a lovely, steady pressure as he strokes it, making circles and then passing over it again, and again, until I'm leaning back into his arms and my legs are trembling underneath me.

But this isn't fair. Why am I almost naked while he gets to keep his clothes on?

I turn around in his arms, forcing him to withdraw his hand. Vincent gives me a quizzical look as I tug on his red tie.

"You next," I tell him, reaching up to untie it. He allows me to do it, hands on my hips as I pull the tie free and toss it aside. His shirt buttons follow, and it seems like Vincent is holding his breath as I work my way from his collar to his belly, untucking the shirt from his pants. Underneath, his green skin pokes out, and I want to see even more. I slide the suit jacket off his shoulders, and he lets it spill down his arms and onto the floor.

"Shirt," I insist, and Vincent agreeably plucks the buttons free on each of his wrists before tugging off the shirt, too.

Now at last, I can see him—and my eyes devour all of it. His pecs are enormous, and it's no wonder they strain his shirts. His powerful belly is almost as thick, his abdominal muscles pulsing with his breaths.

I know what I need to do. I fall to my knees, so his crotch is right in front of me, and begin with the hook on his slacks. Then I pull down the zipper, revealing his dark blue briefs. He's huge and hard underneath, trapped down his thigh. Vincent's watching me intently as I pull down the band, allowing that thick, heavy thing to go free. But before I touch it, I drag his clothes the rest of the way down his massive thighs and bulky calves.

He definitely doesn't skip leg day.

Now his massive cock is released, full of blood and ready for me. I lick the droplet forming at the tip, and Vincent sucks in again. But I've only just begun.

CHAPTER
THIRTEEN

VINCENT

There is nothing quite as magical as your mate kneeling in front of you, sucking on your cock like it's the most delicious lollipop. It's a struggle just to keep my feet underneath me as her lips envelop my cockhead and her hand wraps around the base. She strokes while she licks, taking her sweet time to bring me in deeper.

Fuck. She's going to kill me like this.

I'd intended to get her on the bed and suck her clit until she screamed, but here we are. I'll never turn down a blowjob from a woman as skilled as Rosette.

Just thinking her name makes my balls shiver. *My* Rosette. I will convince her that this is what she is. But I can't do that with my cock in her mouth.

"Rosette," I murmur to her, stroking her hair. She pauses with my length sunk deep in her throat and peers up at me. "Get up on the bed. I want to taste you, too."

Her eyes get bigger. She withdraws me from her mouth, then climbs onto the bed, shucking her underwear in the process. I lie down beside her on my back.

"Put that pussy on my mouth," I say, in a gentler voice than Mr. Roth would use. A wicked smile splits Rosette's face, and she does as she's told, clambering up so she's sitting astride my head. Then she bends forward and sucks my cock back into her mouth.

I turn all my focus toward loving on her cunt, hoping to hold off my own orgasm. She's my mate, and all my cum needs to go inside her, where it belongs.

She's so sweet, so tangy on my tongue, it's all I can do not to pull her down and rub her all over my face. I lick her feverishly, swirling and circling and passing back and forth, tasting and swallowing and licking all over again. Occasionally I put my tongue inside her, lapping her up, before I return to tormenting her clit. I've managed to put the sensation of her mouth on my cock in the background, but now she's doing all kinds of marvelous tricks—suctioning when she pulls me out, caressing me with her tongue, playing with my balls in her little hands—that are taking my attention.

"Rosette." I say her name until she stops sucking me off like a professional. "Get on your back." I swallow, adding, "Please."

She blinks at me over her shoulder, then does as I ask, shuffling to lie down on the bed. When I make love to her, and that's what I'm going to do, I want to be on top of her. I want to see her spread out underneath me, her legs around my waist, her perfect tits bouncing. Then I can hold her close when the time is right and show her what a future with me would be like.

My cock seizes just thinking about it.

I crouch over her, dragging the tip down her soft belly. She has just the right amount of flesh on her, absolutely perfect, with rounded hips and a plush stomach that flexes as she looks down, getting an eyeful of my dick.

As eager as I am to be inside her, I haven't gotten to worship Rosette properly before now, to show her how deeply she affects me. So I drop onto one elbow to kiss her again, reveling in the sweet and silky taste of her, how her lips give and yet dance, pushing and pulling, her tongue teasing mine with a raw sensuality that is uniquely hers.

I have not truly appreciated this yet, and that was a fault on my part. All this time, Rosette has simply been begging for tenderness, for a slow unfurling of her desire, and I have done nothing but take and consume.

Gently, I release her mouth, then continue my kisses down her chin to her jaw and throat. She shudders as I suck on a sensitive part of her neck, and I am tempted to give her a bruise here so that everyone will know she belongs to me.

I need to resist for now. Until she agrees to be my mate and mine alone.

I can't think about what might happen if she doesn't.

At last, I reach her left nipple, and it's peaked and taut for me already. After skimming over it with my palm and drawing a soft gasp from her, I lean down and whirl it into my mouth. Her back arches as I pull on it with my lips, then lick and suck again. Both breasts receive my attention, as flawless as they are. Fuck, how much I would love to spend the rest of my life with my head between these tits.

"Vincent," she whimpers. "Harder!"

"My filthy girl wants it rougher, does she?" I do as I'm told, this time nipping her with my teeth and pulling. She moans, her body rising off the bed to meet me. So I perform the same ritual on the other breast, giving her nipples all my attention until she's panting and grabbing my shoulders.

"Please." She gulps. "I—I need you."

Hearing this lights up every nerve ending in my body. I sit up and pull the foreskin back from my cock. It's leaking noticeably, more than ready to finally consummate this mating.

I shift and spread her thighs until I'm between them, her pussy fully bared to me. She trims it neatly, and I like that she doesn't shave it all. It makes her look like a woman—one that I'm about to claim forever.

Before I move further, though, I reach down to push some hair back behind her ear, then cup her cheek in my palm.

"Rosette."

Her eyes flash up to mine, and the lust in them is palpable.

"I want you to know that I'm yours. I've

been yours for a long time, and I plan to keep it that way." I lean closer, my cock thirsting for nothing more than to be inside her. "I'm going to learn everything about you. And then, once I understand you... I'm going to love you. I'm going to love you so hard that you'll never look anywhere else for it."

She searches my face as if suspicious of what I've said. I kiss her once more, letting everything I feel soak into her, then retreat so I can finally do what I've been dying to do since the very first moment I laid eyes on Rosette.

ROSETTE

I don't recognize Mr. Roth anymore. No, now he's Vincent, the real Vincent, and he's not at all what I expected to lie underneath the gruff and steel. The way his eyes are searching me makes him look truly vulnerable, now that he's put out on the table how he feels about me.

"I've never loved anyone," I finally admit. "But... I am open to learning."

That smile returns, the one that I've only seen for the first time tonight, and Vincent's hand skates down my cheek to my breasts, then my pelvis. He pushes my thighs farther apart, hiking them up over his hips, then takes his cock in his hand.

"First lesson." He huffs with pleasure as he smears his pre-cum all over me. Then he slides down, right to where he belongs, and ever so slowly pushes through.

I gasp at how wide he spreads me with just the head, stretching me open for him as far as I can go. Still mightily aroused from sitting on his face, I feel myself squeezing down at the same time he slides in farther, asking me to open for him.

"Damn," Vincent groans, staring down at where his cock is spearing me. "Your pussy is glorious." He cants his hips back slightly, then shoves himself deeper.

This is different—everything about it is different from fucking on Mr. Roth's desk. Now, Vincent is peering inside me, his yellow eyes with the blown-out pupils staring down into mine as he retreats again, then tests the waters, slowly making his way inside me. No one has ever had sex with me like this before, going slow, holding me steady, controlling every movement of every muscle as carefully as Vincent does. I can't help staring back, drowning in him while he opens me wider and wider.

"This is what mates do," Vincent murmurs as he wades almost up to the hilt on his next thrust, which is agonizingly slow. "Do you feel it?"

I know what he's talking about, this steadily building, blistering flame that threatens to become a bonfire if properly fed. It makes me want to suck him into myself, to surround him, to bring our bodies so close together that we become a single, writhing organism.

"Yes," I whisper. "Yes, I do."

Vincent lowers himself to kiss me, again and again, timing his lips with the movement of his hips. He finally finds his seat, buried in me as far as he can be, and he lets out a sigh of satisfaction.

"Rosette." He says my name like a prayer. "Nothing in the world feels as good as you."

He stays settled deep like that, gently pulling out only a fraction before pushing back in, like he's seeking something out. That small flame takes shape, burning brighter as Vincent makes love to me.

Shit. I know that's what this is, what we're doing, and it makes my soul sing as much as my eyes sting. Who knew this orc was capable of such things, of showing me his heart, when it was buried so deep down inside?

I wrap my arms around his neck and pull him close, burrowing into his shoulder. He cradles my head like that, continuing his steady, rhythmic pace, seeking my pleasure and then drawing it out. Our bodies move in flawless unison, my belly to his, my thighs wrapped around his hips. Each plunge of his cock inside me adds another bit of tinder to the fire until it's blossoming upward and sending showers of sparks shooting up my arms and legs.

"Vincent," I whimper, holding him even closer, if that were possible. "Vincent, please, I... I need to... I'm..." My brain is a jumble of thoughts and feelings and pleasure.

"I've got you." He holds me closer, picking up his speed.

"Ah!" I have no choice. My body is coming apart at the seams, glowing from inside like a star in the midst of a supernova. I cry out, gripping him tight, his cock making obscene noises as it slicks in and out, going deep and then nearly withdrawing, over and over until every part of my skin is shivering. The flame is spreading, growing, billowing up and consuming me, the pleasure so bright it's almost painful.

"Let go, Rosette," he says to me, kissing my hair. "I'll catch you."

So I do. At last, my body releases, and I tighten all over at the same moment that I expel everything. It's like a storm bearing down on me, blowing me over, and the only thing I can cling to is Vincent. I'm screaming as he fucks me through it, and he's groaning my name as he swells inside me. Now my edges strain, trying to contain him, and I ricochet up and down, higher and higher, until I don't know if I can take any more without crumbling to dust.

"All mine." Vincent groans as he slams deep, and his nails dig into my skin. He pumps once, twice more, and already I feel him coating my pussy and spilling out, down my ass. His arm wobbles, and to avoid crushing me, Vincent braces himself on both elbows.

"There you are." He touches his forehead to mine, looking into my face. "I think I see Rosette now."

If I weren't already flushed all over, I would probably blush. I definitely saw Vincent, the orc he really is inside, and I'll never, ever forget it.

CHAPTER
FOURTEEN

ROSETTE

'm awakened by the sound of soft music playing. Then there's a bird call, and slowly, dim light filters into the room.

Right. I'm at Vincent's house. We fell asleep curled around one another last night after the most incredible sex of my life, where we did nothing more than missionary position. Damn.

Now I'm lying under the comforter, curled against Vincent's side and partially resting on top of him, his chest rising and falling under my head with his deep, sleeping breaths. The music continues, growing louder as even more light filters into the room.

Oh. It's... automated. The windows appear to be tinted but are slowly lightening, as if on a timer. I check my watch and sure enough, it's exactly eight a.m., and the bird calls are growing in volume.

"Vincent," I hiss, because he's sleeping right through it. "Vincent, can you wake up and turn off the birds?"

His eyes fly open, and he scrambles to the bedside table to grab a remote. Abruptly, the music and the bird calls stop, and he rubs his eyes.

"Sorry," he says, flopping back down on the pillow. "It takes a lot to wake me up. I like to be... eased into it."

I stifle my laugh. He curls his arm around me and brings me back in to cuddle more, and I can't say I mind. We lie like that for a long time as the room brightens, simply enjoying the feel of one another's warm skin. His hand coasts down my side, and eventually, curls around my ribs so he can cup one of my breasts.

It's not long before we're feverishly kissing again, hands every which way, Vincent's cock growing thick where it's pressed between us.

"Turn around," he murmurs.

I flip over so my back is to his front, and he

lifts one of my thighs so he can get access to me. He feels marvelous from this angle as he slips inside me, remaining shallow as he brushes over my clit with his finger. He gives me just the tip like this, over and over, rubbing me more furiously as I approach my climax.

I'm about to orgasm, and he's not even inside me yet.

"Fuck!" I moan as it rips through me, which is surprising this early in the morning. I'm not usually so sensitive. As my climax courses through my blood, Vincent thrusts in deep, and he groans with satisfaction.

"Milk my cock," he whispers into my ear as he continues pushing through my clenching muscles. "I can't wait to make you come again."

And he does. He makes me come again so hard that I scream and my vision blurs. I squeeze his hand tight in mine, not remembering when we linked them together, as I come back down to earth.

We both lie there, panting, his cum dripping down my thigh. Eventually, Vincent withdraws and offers me a hand.

"Shower?" he asks, leaning down to kiss me.

"Don't mind if I do."

It's a lovely, easygoing Sunday morning together. After a surprisingly chaste shower, where Vincent only kisses me under the warm spray, we towel off and he offers me some of his "smaller" clothes. I only need one of his massive shirts over me to act as, essentially, a dress, and his eyes rove over me with more hunger than I've ever seen on him.

"Something about that," he says, fondling my tits through the thin fabric, "is incredibly hot."

"Oh, wearing my boyfriend's shirt?"

"You mean, your mate's shirt."

I don't answer right away because, truthfully... I still don't believe him. Vincent's changed, but I don't know if I've made the same leap.

Because I worry. I worry what this means for me. What it means for my job as his assistant, for my job at Octavio's. What does being his mate really entail?

"We should talk about that," I say, and his lips thin into a line.

"I see." Vincent leads the way down the stairs to the kitchen, where he quietly starts pulling out a carton of eggs and a package of bacon.

"I didn't think you cooked for yourself," I say, watching him over a mug of coffee.

"I can cook."

It sounds a little defensive, and I wonder if I've hurt his feelings.

He tosses some bread in the toaster, then slathers it with an aioli sauce before adding bacon and eggs.

"Breakfast sandwich," he says as he puts one down in front of me, then takes the seat next to mine. His hand roams up my thigh as we dig in, but then he draws it away again.

God, the sandwich is good, and exactly what I needed after last night. I glance at Vincent from the corner of my eye, and he's focused on the table as he eats. When we're done, he clears the table in silence, and I wish I knew what to say.

I guess we need to figure out our boundaries.

"I want to keep working at Octavio's."

Vincent's head shoots up where he's cleaning the bacon pan.

"But you don't need the money if you're with me," he says, perplexed.

I wish he understood that it wasn't about the money. "I like it. I like... being watched. Being wanted. Being seen."

He puts down the pan and studies me as I talk. His hand flexes into a fist, but then he releases it and his shoulders droop.

"It would be difficult for me," he says, turning his head away. "I want to be the only one to touch you that way. If you... if you decided to be mine."

"I thought so." I pull my legs up onto the chair so I can hug my knees. "I don't want to have sex with anyone else. I know that. I can give you that."

He lifts sad eyes to mine. "Even then, I couldn't stay home knowing what other people might be doing to you. It's against all my instincts."

I nod, understanding. Even if he's not there, he'll worry.

I wish there was a way through this, because I don't want to let go of what I've found here, or what I learned last night.

"What if... what if no one touched?" I ask. "What if they just looked?"

Vincent cocks his head. "Only performing?" He thinks through this. "I don't mind if they look. Then they can appreciate and envy what I have." His pride appears fluffed by this.

Good to know some things haven't changed.

I could always be a dancer. There are other underground clubs, places I could perform. Places where... Vincent could perform with me, if he wanted.

"What if you were there?" I ask, taking his hand in mine. "What if you showed everyone what you have? What's yours?"

He stares at me, not understanding. "Showed them?"

"There are clubs where performers, you know, do things on stage. You could, maybe"—I swallow hard—"fuck me there. Where everyone can see."

His eyes widen. "You would want that?"

The idea is brilliantly exciting. People watching as Vincent claimed me? As his huge cock opened me, as he fondled me and touched me?

"Oh, yes." That would certainly make up for the lack of touching. "Most definitely."

He thinks for a time as he sips his coffee. Then, after a few more minutes, he nods.

"All right. I would do that with you. Only with you. And you cannot be with anyone else."

I expected that much. I lean over to kiss his cheek.

"Yes. Please."

He nods. "Then that's what you'll have."

VINCENT

There is still the matter of Rosette working as my assistant. We both know this can't persist while we're in a relationship of this magnitude— one that I intend to make permanent.

Which will, unfortunately, require a trip to my home. I will have to introduce her to the family, as one does with a new mate, and perform the mating rituals with her there. If that's still what she wants after three months.

That was her timeline. *Let's try it for three months. If it works out, then yes. I'll be whatever you want.*

I am more than happy to wait as long as she needs until I get to keep her at my side.

Yes, I have asked her to move in. No, she has not agreed yet. She is keeping her apartment until after we get "married"—her human word for the mating rituals. Legal marriage will be a separate issue, one that I'm not looking forward to, as it means a human wedding with her friends and family.

I roll my eyes thinking about it, but I will pay for whatever affair she wants. Now, I find I live only to please her, to grant her wishes wherever and whenever they call for me.

Despite the mating exception, human resources will insist on separating us. We both know this, and so right away, after attending to our paperwork, Rosette sets to finding a replacement. I'm loath to see her go, because I have had many other assistants in the past, and none have been so smart and capable as she is.

"Don't worry," she says, squeezing my arm. "I'll find you someone."

And she does manage to find someone—a young man fresh out of school, someone I would never have selected for myself. He's small but surprisingly fiery.

"His boyfriend goes to my gym," she explains. "I think he'll be perfect for you. He's also anal retentive."

I don't like the implication, but I agree to try him out, anyway.

He talks much more than Rosette did, but otherwise I find Collin to be attentive and insightful. Rosette trains him on her job, and I learn much about how she did her work just by overhearing them.

"Always pay attention to what the client *won't* say," she explains. "When Mr. Roth asks a pointed question and they dodge it, it's almost always something we want to watch out for. Usually a hole in their projections."

But now that she's on her way out, where does that leave Rosette? This question gets under my skin. I want the best for her, but it likely means moving to a different department or another firm entirely. I also need her close to me, and I certainly don't want to imagine some other boss of hers looking at her the way I did.

On her last week training Collin, I finally broach the subject.

"We haven't yet discussed what you're doing after this," I say to her one night, while she lies in my bed naked and sweating. It's silly that she hasn't moved in here when she's over every night. I insist on sleeping next to my mate.

She gives me a quizzical look. "Oh. Naomi hired me."

I blanch. "What? How did you—?"

"She approached me right after the gala. She hasn't had a good assistant in years and always thought I did a good job for you."

And here I was, worried about nothing.

"Don't you want a dog, though?" I ask. I had

so hoped I could bribe her into staying home with a new pet.

She thinks about that for a moment. "Well, maybe we can hire a dog nanny?"

I bark out a laugh, and she smiles widely. I like seeing Rosette when she comes out. I love her, actually.

I really, really do.

EPILOGUE

ROSETTE

One of my less bright moves was not looking up orcish mating rituals before I agreed to them. It wasn't until Vincent explained it to me that I learned we would need to wash each other in an ancestral pool in front of all of Vincent's friends and family—and his entire clan.

Oh, and also? Vincent isn't even his real name. It's *Gorak*.

My new husband's real name is Gorak, and I had no idea.

"Vincent's my middle name," he says. And I do remember seeing a document somewhere that said *G. Vincent Roth*.

Our three months go... well, swimmingly. I'm never home, despite the rent I'm paying on my apartment. Vincent encourages me to switch up the art in his house, revealing that he has a small collection to choose from. Every night, he sleeps wrapped around me like he can't imagine letting me go.

Now we go out to eat, and I order my own meal—unless I can't decide, and then he chooses for me. I like being able to hand my choices over to him, and easily he slides in and picks what he knows I really want.

I parted ways with Octavio's, which wasn't as difficult as I'd expected. Not when The Black Cavalier invited me in with open arms to be a performer. I'm sure it helped that Vincent bought a rather large share in the place.

Our first night on stage, Vincent changes. He becomes Mr. Roth again, dressed in his suit and tie, while I'm in revealing "office" attire.

"Filthy slut," he says to me, slapping my ass. He bends me over the swing, rubbing me across the gusset of my panties. "You like your boss fucking you, don't you?"

"Oh, I do, Mr. Sebastian," I say, murmuring

his stage name. "I especially like when he comes inside me."

Vincent makes a growling noise that's all him, clearly ready to get this show on the road.

It's not long before he's unbuckling his belt, which he uses—with my pre-approval, of course—to slap my thighs and ass a few more times.

Then, he puts me onto the swing and spreads my legs wide, turning me so everyone can see as he fists his massive cock and thrusts inside me.

Nothing is as good as dozens of people watching as my mate fucks me. That's what I am, I know it now. He's mine, all mine.

And then there are the nights together. He tells me everything in his silk sheets, and I know before the three months are up what decision I'm going to make.

"Let's do the rituals," I tell him over breakfast one Saturday morning.

Vincent sits upright. "Truly? I can organize it for next week."

"Next week, then. And we can have the wedding later, after we've had some time to plan for it."

Vincent huffs out a breath but nods in agreement, anyway.

He always gives me what I want.

VINCENT

I never really understood orc mating rituals before I participated in one. Now, I think I do.

First, we are separated from each other, which I'm sure makes Rosette nervous among so many strangers. I am stripped down naked and then my peers, orcs I grew up with, are there in the room cleaning me and covering me in fragrant oils. We chat about life in the city, how everything there is busy and fast in comparison to these old mountains.

Then I'm dressed in ancestral attire, the ceremonial kind with many sashes and ornaments, and my mother fusses over me until it's perfect.

"I never thought my hardworking, stoic son would find his forever mate," she says, patting the side of my face. "I am so glad."

Then it's time for the ceremonies. Rosette is sparkling when I see her, hair shining and skin glowing. Braziers are lit, and songs are sung by my clan mates as we stand in the middle and hold hands. Hers are so perfect and small in mine, I want to swallow her up.

Next, I am given some smoking herbs and

must walk around her ten times, binding her soul with mine. Perhaps it is simply the smoke, but it's as if I can feel it working, bringing us even closer together. Gazing down into Rosette's eyes, it's as if the ancient will of my people is guiding us... and I feel a connection to it and to her.

The mating instinct is never wrong.

After the ceremonies, we're led to the ceremonial pools. We undress each other in front of the clan, and then I guide her into the water. There, I wash her clean, and she does the same to me while everyone sits in quiet reverence. When we're finished, a cheer goes up from all the orcs in attendance. We're draped with towels and sent off on our way to consummate our new mating alone.

With one of her legs up over my shoulder, the other cradled in the crook of my elbow, I show Rosette exactly what she means to me.

It will be time soon to meet her parents and siblings, and her best friend from middle school. Then a grand wedding, as appropriate. But I am, to my own surprise, excited about all of it.

Especially the part where I brought home two matching puppies from the shelter and Rosette screamed the loudest, happiest scream I've ever heard. And I make her scream a lot.

She promptly named them Sandwich and Blueberry, because she claims dogs should always have food names and not people names.

And every Saturday night, I dress up as Mr. Sebastian and fuck my woman in front of everyone, showing them she's mine.

All mine.

THANK YOU FOR READING!

I hope you enjoyed Vincent and Rosette's love story. If you did, please consider leaving a review! Reviews are incredibly helpful to authors like me in finding new readers.

JOIN MY NEWSLETTER!

For all the latest regarding books, and to get access to a FREE novella, join my newsletter!

www.LyonneRiley.com

Get lots of steamy art to go with your favorite stories! Visit me on Patreon for my latest ongoing serial.

Patreon.com/LyonneRiley

ABOUT THE AUTHOR

Lyonne Riley published her first book at age five, which was written on tiny sheets of notebook paper, and she insisted on giving a copy to everyone she knew. She's been writing ever since, from fan fiction in her teen years to original fiction as an adult. After a stint in traditional publishing, she discovered what she truly wanted to write: very smutty stories about monsters and the little humans they worship.

Now she lives in the middle of nowhere with her dogs and spouse, writing sexy fairy tales.

ACKNOWLEDGMENTS

I would like to thank everyone involved in helping me through the process of putting out this book. I can't say enough how much I appreciate the help and encouragement of the people around me—especially Amber, who told me I could do this in the first place.

Huge thank you to Rowan Woodcock for the gorgeous cover illustration. A big thank you to Ana Hansen of Sparks Editorial. To my critique partners, who gave me phenomenal feedback: You all make this possible. And of course, my amazing spouse, who has always supported my dreams—and given me lots of inspiration for my characters' sexy adventures.

I couldn't have done this without the expertise of my fellow self-published romance authors. Thank you for inviting me into your circles and helping me through this process.

And thank you to my readers, who gave this book a shot.